BE A SEX-WRITING STRUMPET

D1366412

Introduction

Hi there!

In the late spring of 2008 I was a bit at loose ends. My new agent and I were working on edits for my novel UNHOLY GHOSTS, and I was holding off on starting any new projects until it had been submitted and--hopefully--bought (which it was, by Del Rey in the US and HarperVoyager in the UK, and the first book was released 5/25/10). Meanwhile, I'd stopped writing straight romance--I'd come to believe my voice just didn't quite suit it. I'd already turned in the second Demons novel and completed edits on it, as well.

So I was kind of adrift, as far as new projects went. Meanwhile summer was coming and I was itching to do another "Summer Series" on my blog to follow up my 2007 Summer Series on choosing and evaluating small publishers.

During the course of some random wanderings around the internet I found a discussion of one of my sex scenes, which inspired a blog post, which got me thinking. Despite essentially leaving romance, I still loved to write sex scenes, and still felt confident about them. And that perhaps I had some thoughts and opinions and tips to share on writing them.

So I asked my blog readers if they'd be interested in such a series. The response was overwhelmingly positive, and we got started. The entire series lasted from July 9th-- September 17th, 2008, and comprised thirty-one blog posts, of which six were critiques (which are not reproduced here) and one was a guest blog (also not reproduced here; both can still be found on the blog itself).

I've gotten more email from this series than any other post I've ever done. I still get emails about it, in fact, and requests to offer it as a PDF or book. Unfortunately, my lack of techie skills started to make me think I'd never be able to do that. Sigh.

But enter uberwriter James D. MacDonald, and his awesome computer-fu, and his offer to format somebody's work for them, and we're in business. Huge, enormous thanks to him for doing this, and to all of you for reading it and letting me know how much it helped you.

Stace

Part One: What does a sex scene do?

Okay. Before we begin...as always, the little disclaimer. This series is about how *I* write sex/love scenes. It is *not* about the best way or the only way; it's about *MY* way. I assume if you're reading it, it's because you read my blog and therefore have at least a passing familiarity with me and/or my work (although that's not necessary) but, more to the point, that you actually find my sex scenes enjoyable and arousing and are therefore here to get some insight on them and how I write them, and what I've learned from writing them. In other words, I assume we have some general basis for agreement about what is hot in a sex scene. If you don't like my sex scenes, why are you here? Seriously. We will also be touching upon a few of the things I wrote about in my Heroes series, specifically the bits on chemistry. I'll link to those when we get to them.

So. Writing sex scenes. How about that, huh? In my mind, a sex scene has four main purposes:

1. **It shows us something about the character(s).**

2. **It shows us something about the relationship.**

3. **It advances the story.** (there is a subrule here. We'll call it 3a, and it is **It increases tension**. Sounds kind of funny, because you'd think of it as a release of tension, but we'll get into that later.)

4

4. **It arouses the reader.** (Note: I am speaking specifically about sex scenes in romance/erotic romance/urban fantasy with romantic elements/erotica. I will later deal with sex scenes that don't have this element, but for now, this is where our focus is so this is what the purpose of our sex scenes is. Okay?)

That seems like an awful lot for one sex scene to cover, doesn't it? Especially the bit about advancing the story, because let's face it. There are lots of critics out there who claim romance or erotic romance is just a tiny story with a bunch of sex thrown in to pad it out. They're wrong (at least they should be; we've all read books like those, but do you really want to write them?).

And here's why. Because in a romance/erorom/romantic uf, part of the story, be it large or small, IS the relationship. How is it possible for two people to have sex and it changes absolutely nothing about their relationship? How is it possible for us as readers to "see" them together in the most intimate of situations and not know something more about them, not see their relationship change? How is it possible for us as writers to ignore the impact of that?

It's not. No matter what, once your characters have had sex, their relationship changes. Irrevocably. Actually, their relationship should change with every conversation, every casual touch, every glance, every kiss, even if it's not readily apparent. But it is impossible for your characters to have sex and not see each other differently afterward. And that is one of the "jobs" of the sex scene, to show that relationship actually changing (before the reader's very eyes! Just like one of those magic sponges that swells in the tub. Something should certainly be swelling in a sex scene, anyway. Heh heh.)

So. We know what a sex scene needs to do. If it doesn't do those four things, it doesn't belong in the book. This is true even for the most sex-filled erotic romances. If the sex isn't exploring, defining, and advancing plot, character, and relationship, it needs to go away. And in an erotic romance or a regular romance, you have a lot of room to maneuver in those strictures.

A brief example: When final edits on *Blood Will Tell* were complete, it went to the final readers, who gave the book a rating of "S," or "Sensual." (Ellora's Cave has since changed their ratings, btw.) S books are fine, of course, but they don't sell as well as E-rated (Erotic) or higher. I was given a choice. Sell it as S, or add more sex. It wasn't a difficult decision. But it was difficult figuring out where to add the scenes. I finally came up with two: the pool scene, and one of the hotel scenes (the one where Julian wakes up Cecelia). Now, adding sex is all well and good, but I had to figure out how to do all four things with each scene. Where did those areas need to be expanded?

It took me several days to hit on it, but I did. The new pool scene shows several things: How Julian feels about a decision he's made, which up to then the reader hasn't understood was a serious and drastic decision to make. In showing that, it also shows how important Cecelia has become to him.

It gives us an insight into her understanding of him, and his respect for her opinion (a big deal for someone used to being in charge and ignoring other people's opinions). It adds tension both by showing Julian lying yet again to hide his true nature and by showing their relationship grow increasingly close—and both of those things also advance the story. Finally, hopefully it was damn hot. I sure thought it was when I wrote it, and it remains one of my favorite scenes in the book.

The other addition, the hotel scene, works in a different way. It brings Julian's guilt into clear focus and allows the reader to see what exactly is holding him back. It's the first time he admits to himself what his true feelings are. In doing those things, of course, it jumps the story—remember, the story here is ABOUT their relationship, and everything else is secondary—forward. Is it arousing? Well, I think so, but it's certainly not the hottest scene in the book by any stretch. It's not particularly explicit. But if I did my job, it aroused the reader because of those emotions and feelings.

This isn't to say, though, that an erotic romance has to be about sex. I've grown tired of the "magic vajayjay" conceit, whereby the heroine heals people or gains power through sex, and thus has sex with numerous partners, or one partner numerous times, purely as a sort of exercise of strength. That doesn't mean it can't still work, but I think readers are becoming jaded by it; it's regarded as lazy and silly now (and the "magic vajayjay" applies also to those stories where the base healing power of sex is overblown to the point where one good bed session heals all the hero/ine's hang-ups and emotional problems. Be very careful about keeping change realistic).

So. Next time we'll start getting into mechanics. I have a LOT of material planned.

Whee! I'm really excited about this! We're going to spend a few days examining the purpose/timing/etc of sex scenes--the basic stuff--and then move into the mechanics of voice, language, rhythm, dialogue, setting, characterization, all that stuff. Along the way I think we'll have a really good time.

Part 2: Do you need a sex scene?

Before we get into the nitty-gritty of writing a sex scene that will arouse, educate, and (heh heh) inspire your readers, and will advance so many things in your book itself, we should contemplate whether or not we need a sex scene at all. Not in the "Should they have sex here" sense (that will be covered in part on Wednesday when we start talking about chemistry), but in the sense of "Do I actually need to write sex? Couldn't I just fade out from a kiss?"

Well. My feelings on this are strong, and perhaps not popular in all circles. And I'm well aware that there are some subgenres in romantic fiction that frown on sex scenes—Inspirational, for example. Of course if you and/or your readers believe strongly that premarital sex is wrong, and your book ends before the wedding, you wouldn't even contemplate writing a sex scene. And there's nothing wrong with that. Mostly. (Really.) But if you're writing Inspirationals, you're probably not hanging around my potty-mouthed corner of the internet, right?

I don't particularly care for those who get loud and nasty about it, and denigrate myself and other erotic writers as filthy smut-peddlers (I enjoy being called a filthy smut-peddler, but not in a *mean* way). I get irritated and angry when it's time for the bi-yearly "Romance with sex in it isn't REAL romance" debate, courtesy of some RWA letter or writer's blog or whatever. (Because there is apparently nothing remotely romantic about the joining of two bodies into one, especially not in the most literal sense when the act creates another human being; when people call it "making love" they do so in the spirit of bitterest irony. Don't get me wrong, it doesn't have to be romantic—I kind of like it best when it's not, actually—but the idea that it never can be is ridiculous.)

And I admit, any variation of the sentiment or phrase "Writing sex is for people who can't write WELL" or "Writing sex is a cop-out and takes no skill and is catering to the lowest common denominator" or "Writing sex is easy" or "If you have to resort to writing sex to sell your work then there's a weakness in your writing skills" (yes, I've heard all of those, once to my face, even) absolutely infuriates me. I wouldn't be doing this little series/workshop/whatever if sex was easy to write, guys. I wouldn't have already heard from several well-published, very good, successful professional writers that they're glad I'm doing this because they have difficulty writing sex scenes. Sex is NOT easy to write. I truly believe writing a good sex scene is a challenge, no matter how many you've written. It's disrespectful beyond measure to dismiss the work of another writer in that fashion; it's extremely rude and it's just a nasty, mean thing to say.

Okay, rant over, sorry. Let's move on. The question here is whether the sex scene is actually necessary, and whether you can do without it, and here's my take on that: If you can find another way to illuminate the most private acts of your characters, to demonstrate their connection, their trust, the depth of their feelings (or lack thereof; we'll cover that later too), their desire for each other, the moment their relationship deepens and changes beyond anything they've been through before, while also strengthening the story, increasing tension, and adding complications, and also— let's be honest here—giving the reader what they've been waiting for, and you can do all of that in one scene, then no, you don't need the sex scene.

But since the sex scene must do all of those things, and since in order to be effective the sex scene should be the only thing that does all of those things...well, we start to go in circles now, don't we?

I am a firm believer in putting sex in books. I'm for it; there's really no other way to put it. I love writing sex scenes. I like reading sex scenes. I wait for sex scenes. And yeah, I get rather unhappy when the door is closed in my face. Because you can tell me the characters had sex all you want. You can show me how they smile at each other, or how they touch hands at breakfast, or whatever. But the fact is, if you haven't given me the sex scene, it feels like *telling*. You've deliberately excluded me from something, something I as a reader feel entitled to. I've waited two hundred fifty pages or whatever for these characters to act on their feelings, and you're going to show me a couple of kisses then fade to black? But...but what did they *do*? What did they say? How did they look at each other, what did they feel, how did they touch each other? How did their feelings change? How do you plan to show me all that stuff without the sex scene?

As writers we pick and choose what our readers see, of course. It's boring otherwise; we don't need to write every minute of their every day. I personally don't care to read about or write about the toilet habits and experiences of characters—but you can bet your ass that if it was important to the story, I would, whether I liked it or not.

And far more than that, there's an implication I really dislike when the bedroom door is closed. I've mentioned before my distaste for people who run around making films or writing books to "illuminate" the concept that sex is a profound human experience and that while having it we are vulnerable or we are our true selves or whatever. My distaste isn't for that idea; it's for the idea that in saying sex is a profound human experience blah-blah-blah we're somehow saying something clever and original. Um, duh.

BUT. Sex *is* a profound human experience—or at least, it damn well should be, especially in romantic fiction. The mere act itself *should* change us, shake us, make us see ourselves and/or our partner differently. So I strongly, strongly resent the subtle (or not-so-subtle) implications of those sex-scene naysayers, which are: that sex isn't about people and relationships but is merely a distasteful biological imperative; that it doesn't involve hearts or minds or souls but only sticky engorged naughty parts; that sex really isn't important; *that every couple in the world has sex the exact same way* ; that it shows us nothing of importance about ourselves or each other and therefore does not need to be part of the story.

The dirty underside of that stick is a sort of contempt for readers, in the idea that they don't deserve to see the characters' private moments, that such times are either too good and special for the likes of them—as if our characters are real people who will look up from their bed of sin and shriek and pull the covers over themselves, and the reader is nothing but a nosy, interfering houseguest who doesn't know when to leave the room— or worse, that the reader is a perverted busybody for daring to even be interested in such things, that wanting to know the characters and their relationship as thoroughly as possible is somehow wrong of us. We're filthy voyeuristic beasts, you see, those of us who expect to be treated like adults instead of like Pittypat Hamilton or something. Good thing we have the author there to keep our dirty little minds out of the gutter, where presumably all manner of revolting deeds are occurring, too distasteful and gross for the writer to detail for us. Oh, they'll let us know it happened, but the event itself is simply too icky to detail.

And that's crap. We should be seeing it, because it's important to see it.

**Um, at least most of the time. There is a small exception, and that is when the characters in question are involved in a steady sexual relationship and this is not an erotic romance. For instance, although Greyson and Megan spend a good chunk of the time period covered by *Demon Inside* doing delightful things in bed with each other, only two of those scenes are detailed. The first because it gives the reader a good look into where their relationship is at the start of the book, and the second because, IMO, it jumps both relationship and story forward by a huge bound (and is hopefully scorching hot too.) So I will give you a pass for later books in series or second, third, fourth, etc. encounters that don't significantly expand or change the relationship or affect the story.

But dammit... **If you can honestly tell me that your characters having sex isn't an important enough moment for the reader to share, then your characters shouldn't be having sex at all.**

Next we're going to start looking at chemistry and building anticipation, and then we'll begin with the real mechanics.

Part 3: Writing sex without embarrassment

I wasn't going to post this today. I planned to do more on what a sex scene is actually about, as part of the move into what lies behind a sex scene, after which we begin really working. BUT. It occurred to me I hadn't really left a spot for this subject, and I think it's an important one. Because embarrassment seems to be one of the main reasons people are uncomfortable with writing sex, or dislike writing sex. Because if someone is comfortable writing sex embarrassment seems to be a reason why they aren't comfortable taking their sex scenes beyond a certain point. And because I just think it's a good one to discuss, and this is my series dammit.

Now, there's nothing wrong with modesty or discomfort. Those of you who are regular readers know that I generally keep things on the blog at a certain level (I think of it as "one-cocktail adult", actually—a little looser than normal but not throwing-panties-at-chandeliers), and that there are some things I simply won't write about in my actual work because for one reason or another I find them overly crude or unappealing. This doesn't mean there's anything wrong with those who do, just that I have a certain line in my head that I don't cross—or haven't yet, anyway. (And later on I'll be talking more about writing hot sex scenes without being graphic at all.)

But this is the biggest thing to remember, and it's easy to remember it when you're writing, say, a werewolf with cynophobia but seems much harder when it comes to sex, as sex is literally much closer to home; it's writing what you know in the most intimate sense. *Your characters are not you.* I know, I know. Again, it seems very basic. But I have honestly stopped and reminded myself of this on several occasions, when a scene is moving in a direction I'm not particularly comfortable with.

For example, let's take anal (Please! Ba-dum-bum). The vast majority of my heroines—the vast majority of heroines in erotic romance, really—take great pleasure in all things rear-end. If it's not actual anal sex (which I've only written in three books, two of which were ménages), it's various fingers and other implements. Because it can be arousing to read and because I know a lot of readers find it so. But in real life? Eh. I have on occasion in the past been with men who enjoyed doing such things to me and I have on occasion permitted them to do so. Most men who enjoy doing those things to me enjoy having those things done to them and I have on occasion obliged them (within reason; if you're picturing strap-ons you've gone way too far in your head. Not that there's anything wrong with that, it's just not me). I can take it or leave it, to be honest, but I think if you read my work (particularly *Eighth Wand*, which has far more anal play than any of my other books) you might imagine me as some sort of anal goddess, complete with an array of toys. I'm not.

Nor have I ever been in any sort of ménage. I have never been sexually involved with another woman. I've never had sex in the middle of the day in a public park; I've never, tame as it may sound, engaged in mutual masturbation with a partner. Sex in the shower makes me too hot and I have to go lie down in a cool room for half an hour to keep from passing out (I'm very sensitive to heat), so it's not something I enjoy. But I've written all of those things and more (we're going to look particularly at

14

the mutual masturbation scene from Eighth Wand later in the series, as I'm quite proud of it), and found them arousing to write and arousing to read later (although reading my own work never has the same effect on me as reading other writers' does, because I'm always trying to edit it).

It seems rather silly, doesn't it? Nobody looks at me or reads one of my books and pictures me at home being bitten by vampires or having sex with resurrected Druids or tattooed Fae warriors. But for some reason they do think that I try and like everything I write. So I have to keep in mind at all times that the scene is not about me, it's about my characters; and that to pull them back from where they want to go because of my own modesty or whatever is wrong. It doesn't serve the story. It doesn't serve the characters. And that's not good.

So how do you get beyond that embarrassment? How do you get those words on the page even if you're blushing, or picturing your mom (or worse, your dad) or great-uncle Edwin or your kid's teachers reading it, and imagining you at home in a leather peek-a-boob corset watching porn and, I don't know, smearing whipped cream all over your body? Here's some ideas:

1. **Remember, your characters are not you.** Their fantasies are not necessarily yours; you aren't entirely responsible for their kinks (or lack thereof. And yes, of course we'll cover sex as expansion of characterization).

2. **Plan ahead.** Before I've even started the book, before the chemistry between my characters starts simmering, I'm already beginning to see the sex scene in my head. And I think this really helps. We're going to do more on chemistry on Friday, but if I'm picturing them having sex in my head from the very first moment they meet, I firmly believe it helps add that frisson of heat to

every interaction. Plus, if you're nervous, it gives you lots of time to work out the bugs, as it were.

3.   **Make everybody wait.** Now in an erotic romance you don't have as much time to do this, as you want to get to the sex much earlier. But in a straight romance or another genre with romantic elements... There's a reason why most sex scenes take place about 2/3 of the way through the book, and it's because you want everybody eagerly anticipating. Especially you.

4.   **Write a good kissing scene and interrupt it.** Good sex doesn't appear out of nowhere. You don't have to use the scene, but you should write it. Write a few of them. Anything to get you and the characters amped up enough that none of you want to wait any longer.

5.   **Watch a sexy movie.** Really. Give it a try.

6.   **Have a drink.** See above. If you need a little loosening up, that's fine. Remember, you can edit everything later. Funnily enough, while I think sex scenes are among the hardest to write I find them the easiest by far to edit. Sex scenes develop their own rhythm; it's easy to remove stuff that misses the beat and easy to add things in where a beat is needed.

7.   **Play some music.** I've never really done this; I have on occasion listened to my ipod while writing but I've never, say, put on some Barry White albums before writing sex. Some people swear by such things, though, and I do admit I have a few songs on my ipod that make me think of sex (Nine Inch Nails's cover of "Get Down Make Love" is one; The Stooges's "I Wanna Be Your Dog" is another, along with some Bill Withers. Hey, I think they're very sexy).

16

8. **Think about sex.** Think about good sex or bad sex or funny sex or sad sex or whatever, about sex you've had and sex your friends have told you about. What? It may sound odd, sure, but just the act of thinking about it—reminding yourself that just about every adult on the planet either does it regularly or has in the past—might help to reassure you that you're not about to embark on some bizarre and creepy dark journey of the soul. You're writing about something you've experienced in more ways than one; you're writing about something universal.

9. **Write about something that isn't sex.** Make it as sexy as you possibly can. Again, yes, I'm serious. For example, let's see what sort of sexy things I can say about my couch.

The tawny fabric makes my hand tingle when I rub it, letting the velvety fibers scrape the delicate skin of my palm. Tiny furrows hold cool air, release it like a whisper at my finger's tender command. I rub a little faster, a little harder, the desperate friction between my hand and the glorious softness beneath it growing, until I can't take anymore. I stop, my breast heaving with excitement, my heart pumping, arm and palm aching from the frantic movements.

Okay, it's not a love poem. It's not great; as you all know 1st person isn't my thing and I literally wrote this in a minute. But you get the point, which is to look for sexy words and use them (yes, of course, we'll be doing that too). To think of what each movement is and describe it by feeling as much as by actual act.

Trust me, once you've written a sexy paragraph about your potato peeler (oh! The shiny curved handle so hard and heavy in your hand, its swollen ridges digging into your soft palm, the sharp, cruel slicing blade—merciless in its assault, ruthless against the delicate skin of the potato, exposing the pale flesh beneath!), it'll seem much easier to make actual sex sound sexy.

10. **Read some sexy scenes.** It will inspire you. Read lots of sexy scenes. Find a few you really like and read them before you write any sex scenes. You don't want to copy them, no, but seeing how other people handle them might help relax you. You admire those writers, right? And they can do it, so you can too.

11. **Have your characters discuss their feelings.** Be as cheesy as you like, but no action. Just a dialogue. Now, take all those things they've just discussed and write the sex scene with those things in mind; instead of saying these things they'll be expressing them physically. Instead of saying "I'm afraid you won't be around in the morning," your heroine is hesitant when she lets her fingers play up the hero's chest. Instead of saying "I'm not sure I'm good enough for you," the hero is reverent when he removes the heroine's shirt, or when he dips his head to her breasts, or whatever. Your dialogue is just there to remind you what this scene is really about (and this will be covered extensively later.)

Remember, a sex scene is just a scene, only with naughtyparts. Think about what you want this scene to say about your characters and get it on the page.

You're telling their story, after all. Not your own.

Part 4: When should you write a sex scene?

Q. When is the right time to put a sex scene into your ms?

A. When your characters need to have sex.

Notice I said "need." Now, they can *need* to have sex for any number of reasons. In *Blood Will Tell*, Julian needed to seduce Cecelia so he could drink her blood and find out if she was a spy, and sex was the easiest way to do that. In *Eighth Wand*, Royd needed to seduce Prudence because she had the wand he'd been sent to earth to retrieve, and he'd struck up a bargain with her: a night of pleasure in exchange for the wand.

Conversely, Cecelia needed to have sex with Julian, Prudence needed to have sex with Royd, Santos and Yelina, and Greyson and Megan, and any number of other couples I've written over the years, needed to have sex with each other because they really, really wanted to. Because for whatever reason, and whatever their circumstances were, they wanted each other. Bad. (This is, incidentally, another problem I have with the "magic hoo-ha"; it gives the heroine an "excuse" to have sex with the hero, thus removing responsibility from her decision. If she can't slip off her big-girl panties and say "Yeah, you know what, I really want to fuck this guy," then I'm not that interested in her.)

Notice also I said "need" for other reasons. Perhaps you need your characters to have sex because they're going to discover something about each other during the act that will have major implications on the story and/or plot. If, for example, Heroine has been searching for the man she thinks killed her father, and all she knows about him is that he has a birthmark in the shape of an elephant on his thigh, and our hero just happens to have a birthmark like that... Well, sure, she could catch him in his underwear, or wearing a pair of short shorts, or something, but let's not lose focus on the rest of the work we're doing when writing a story, which is ratcheting up tension. You tell me which is more likely to involve the reader emotionally: When the Heroine sees Dumbo grinning at her from the thigh of a guy she thinks is kind of hot, or when she sees Dumbo grinning at her from the thigh of the man sleeping next to her on well-used sheets, just when she thinks she may have gotten everything she ever wanted? Yeah. I thought so.

All of these are valid reasons for a sex scene. ANY reason can be a valid reason for a sex scene, as long as you've done your job and made me as a reader *believe* it. In *Demon's Triad*, Aleeza is willing to have sex with a total stranger in the middle of the woods. Kind of crazy, right? But (hopefully) you believe it, because you've learned enough about the poor girl by then to know that she's been under a celibacy curse since birth and is so sexually frustrated she's risked her life—almost literally—just to have one orgasm. But whatever the reason, and whatever the situation, your sex scene will not fly if your characters have no chemistry. If your readers aren't at least half as desperate to see these characters have sex as the characters themselves are to have it, your scene will fall flat, no matter how well-written it is. (Or rather, it might not fall flat, but it won't be everything it could be.)

At this point you might want to go back and reread this post from my Heroes series (http://www.staciakane.net/2008/02/14/what-makes-a-hero-part-3-what-do-we-notice-about-him/), which outlines a few ways to create chemistry between your leads. It's more hero-oriented, but it's a good basis for what I'm about to elaborate on.

So how do you make it clear—through SHOWING, not telling—that your characters are dying to hop into bed? How do you make the reader desperate to see it?

In the Heroes post I mention the importance of knowledge about each other. You want to show the reader, beneath the dialogue, beneath the clandestine looks and casual touches, that these people have a connection. Knowing something about the other person is a good way to do this—it's one of my favorite "tricks" to use, because, honestly, it's very important to me in real life and is something I firmly believe is the basis of a real, strong relationship.

The following are all suggestions, nothing more. You can use all of them, or some of them, or come up with your own, or whatever. *I don't mean to even come close to suggesting that there's some sort of paint-by-numbers way to create chemistry, not at all.* Just that these are *ideas.* They're merely here to help you begin thinking about how your characters interact, and to help you begin, with the very first meeting of these characters, to build up your sex scene. You didn't think a sex scene was just about that one scene, did you? Nooo.

A sex scene is the culmination of everything the hero/heroine have done, said, and been through together from the moment they meet (or the moment the reader meets them).

So here you go. Mix, match, or ignore as you will—but I bet you'll find at least a few of these in every romance or romantic subplot you've ever read. They're in no particular order; some are obvious, some less so. These moments can be as subtle or important as you like; it's your book and your characters, after all. This is just to get you thinking. This series isn't about how to write sex exactly the way I do, with the exact level of heat and graphic-ness. It's about how to find the place where *you're* comfortable, how to best serve *your* story and characters within the confines of your own voice and your own vision.

*H/h notice something special about each other, and comment on it, with uncomfortable or pleasing results depending on who they are/where in the relationship they are/etc.

*H/h touch casually. Maybe they feel sparks, or warmth, or comfort? Maybe the hand in theirs or the arm beside theirs is surprisingly strong? Maybe skin is rough or smooth or soft or hard?

*H/h notice how each other smell. Smell is extremely important in human sexual response, thanks to pheromones (http://en.wikipedia.org/wiki/Pheromones). This is quite literally chemistry. It's one reason why we take an instant liking or disliking to some people; it's why that handsome hunk doesn't really turn you on but the slightly nerdy guy beside you does. Do NOT neglect smell. You don't have to be obvious about it. You can slip it in anywhere. But letting the reader know these people like the way each other smells is, in my mind, a necessity.

*H/h find themselves in close quarters; one or both feels awkward. Or aroused. Or both.

*H/h open up to each other, sharing stories or secrets they don't usually share. Maybe they don't know why they're telling each other this? Maybe it's because they have to, for whatever reason. Maybe they're afraid of how the secret will be received, and find it's received with exactly the sort of reaction they were subconsciously/secretly/not-so-secretly hoping for.

*H/h think about sex with each other. Yeah, it's pretty basic, and for that reason I dislike it intensely when this one is overused. The level of use that equals overuse varies with every story, of course, but there are so many more subtle ways to show attraction. While this one shouldn't or needn't be ignored, it's not—absolutely NOT—a substitute for any other kinds of interaction.

*H/h think of each other in a non-sexual way; perhaps they do it without knowing why? Why would you wish for the company of someone you don't trust, for example? Because there's chemistry, that's why.

*H/h flirt. Oh, yes. Flirt away. Let them joke and laugh together. Let them make subtle comments to each other, it doesn't have to be obvious. It doesn't have to be all the time. But this is another extremely important one.

*H/h are unaccountable nervous around each other. Or unaccountably calm.

*One of the two makes a move. How it's received is up to you, but there's nothing wrong with having one character make it clear they want the other (just be careful about sliding into stalkery or crude territory, which is one of the most common if not *the* most common beginner errors) or both characters make clear they want the other.

*They kiss. Yeah, it's an obvious one. It's also a great one. There's a reason why they call those little bits of food they give you before the main meal "appetizers"; it's because they get you wanting more.

*They find they have a similar hobby/interest/whatever.

*There's jealousy when another person with some claim to the other shows up.

*They have dreams/fantasies about the other. This is an oldie, so old it now borders on lame and obvious. Be careful with it, but it is still possible to find a way to use it if it fits the story and/or characters.

*They have extreme—or what feels extreme to them— physical reactions to being around each other/touching each other.

*They make each other feel good. Doesn't have to be all the time. Doesn't have to be "weeping with joy" good. But they lighten each others' moods. They make each other smile. They don't have to understand it. They can be annoyed by it or scared by it or whatever. They don't even have to realize why they feel so good. But it should be there.

*They care about each other. Again, this can be as subtle or as obvious as you like. And it depends on what sort of scene you're writing and what the relationship between the characters is. But it's one to think about.

Now that's a long list. And it's by no means exhaustive. But what it boils down to, what it all ultimately means, is this:

Your Hero/heroine should *react to* and *interact with* each other. If they don't do that, nobody's going to be interested in seeing them have sex.

I think we're all done with theory; next time we'll start getting into practical application.

Part 5: Mechanics: The Language of Sex

I've been debating exactly where the series should go next. On the one hand I think perhaps we should get right into heavy examples and illustrations of how to bring more heat, emotion, character, etc. into your sex scenes. On the other...you have to learn to walk first, right?

All of you write. I'm sure most of you are excellent writers. I know several of you reading this series are writers whose books I've read, and been completely blown away by them, which makes me feel a little silly even doing this at all.

But as I mentioned before, we'll start heavy work next week (I think) so I decided this was as good a time as any.

Sex scenes have a rhythm and mood all their own, and as we all know, the way to create rhythm and mood is through word choices. The way to make your sex scene both fit into the rest of the book and stand out from it is through word choice. Sexy scenes should use sexy words. How sexy they are—how graphic they are—is entirely up to you, because you're the one writing the book. But they must fit the rest of the story. There's nothing more jarring than reading a book where the most offensive word used is "ass" and then coming to the sex scene to discover cunts and cocks flying everywhere. It doesn't fit; it feels like the sex scene has been imported from an issue of *Penthouse*.

This doesn't mean you have to go the other direction, though, and start in with the overwrought euphemisms. Nobody needs to read about purple-headed warriors and oleaginous tunnels of love. (Which, ew.) So here is a list, by level of graphic-ness (and there's some overlap there, so I'm starting with the most and working down to the least; your opinion may vary by a few places one way or the other):

Female Body Parts:

Cunt clit tits slit pussy tunnel channel cleft sex nipples breasts peaks mounds mound (not breasty mounds; the Mounds of Venus) crevice secret place secret folds secret flesh loins entrance treasure "between her legs/thighs" "bundle of nerves" (for clitoris; I also use "her most sensitive spot" on occasion and feel just fine about it) (I deliberately left out "vulva" because I think it is one of the least sexy words ever, as is "crotch.") We also have some historical variations, like cunny, quim, slash, that sort of thing. And of course the more vulgar euphemisms like "hair pie" or "fish taco" or something, which, if you want to use phrases like those in your sex scenes you're reading the wrong series.

Male Body Parts:

Prick balls dick shaft sac penis stalk column sex thickness erection hardness hard length manhood "himself" (as in "he worked himself" or "he shoved himself into her") "between his legs/thighs" "sword" (can be used in a historical, but only in dialogue, I think)

In a class of its own:

Cock

I'm sure there are more. But these are the ones I use most often, the ones I'm most comfortable with and the ones I think most readers will be the same with.

There's a reason why I put "cock" in a class of its own; once a no-no, it's become commonplace enough, I think, that it can be used in almost any sex scene, from the brief and euphemistic to the intense, long, and graphic. Cock doesn't surprise me anywhere I see it; much like a black v-necked top, cock seems to work anywhere. Cock is the new black.

But the thing is, all those Body Part Words, while fun (and while I knew if I didn't list them y'all would be sorely disappointed in me) are only a small part of the scene, and only a very small part of the language choices you'll make.

I call the words I tend to use in sex scenes "trigger" words. While obviously every word we use in writing is carefully chosen and designed to mean exactly what it must and add to mood and feeling etc. etc., in a sex scene you want visceral words. You want words that evoke...well, that evoke SEX. Words like desperate. Aching. Need. Thrust. Caught. Throb. Trembling. Eased. Stroke. Forceful. Powerful. Burn. Fill. Radiated. Pooled. Grip. Bite. Rammed. Velvet. Iron. Tease. Taste. Slip. Flesh. Slid. Ruthless. Bathed. Wet. Slick. Exposed. Glistening. Enflamed. Delicate. Rough. Turgid. Swollen. Feast. Suck. Hard. Swirl. Curve. Round. Engulfed. Exploded. Hungry. Starved. Dancing. Shaking. Thundered. Raw. Pounding. Bruising. Gasping. Tumescent. Friction. Quivering. Penetrate.

Let's make up an example (actually, you could look at my potato peeler or couch bits from Wednesday—did you see the evocative words? Flesh. Exposed. Ridged. Etc.) This is a deliberately bland and lame example, but we're just illustrating one point with it:

Bob set Jane onto the bed and lay down on top of her. Without a word he put his cock into her.

Yuck, right? It sounds like...well, I don't even know what's that bad. But let's take exactly the same lines, without changing anything more than a few words (we're not adding the important emotional physical etc. stuff yet) and read it again:

Bob *threw* Jane onto the bed and *lunged* on top of her. Without a word he *thrust* his *aching* cock into her.

It's still not great, of course, because it was awful to begin with. I'm particularly bothered by the way both sentences end with "her." I itch to fix it, and to add some sense stuff so the action doesn't exist in such a terrible vacuum. But you see here how the use of trigger words changes this from really bland and awful to something with at least a frisson of heat. Thanks to "threw" and "lunged" Bob doesn't seem like some sort of drunken rutting asshole but instead is perhaps more of a desperate Alpha. He's not "putting" his cock into her, like a peg into a board under the watchful eyes of a dozen clipboard-wielding scientists; he's *thrusting* into her, *thrusting* with his *aching, needy* cock. (Yeah, I didn't add needy before, because I think aching makes it obvious there, or would in the context of an entire scene.)

None of this is new to you, because you're writers. So you're familiar with the need for active verbs and forceful words. But where a regular scene might be able to get away with the occasional bland or basic sentence, every word in a sex scene must contribute to the eroticism of the scene. Use the sexiest words you can.

The thing is, in any other part of your book, embellishment is frowned on. You don't need two or three adjectives to describe, say, somebody's cell phone, or their hands or their eyes. You don't need several adjectives to describe someone aiming their gun or pulling the trigger, or running. It would sound overwritten and a bit silly to string words upon words in a regular action scene.

But a sex scene isn't just any action scene. Your words need to evoke a physical and emotional reaction in the reader; it's less about what the characters are doing than about making your reader FEEL what they're doing.

As this section goes on we'll cover adverbs and keeping scenes in tone with the rest of the story, and a little about what to call the, ah, products of orgasm and arousal. Next week I think we'll start adding emotion etc., including dialogue. After that will be foreplay, and one or two other bits, here and there.

So your assignment now, should you choose to accept it, is to make a list of, or at least think about, your own trigger words. What words feel/sound sexy to you? What words do you like to use for body parts? What words evoke certain emotions or feelings appropriate for some sex scenes but not others, and what words work in regular action scenes but wouldn't work in a sex scene (I can think of one off the top of my head: clipped)? Keep hold of that list, and try using those words in your sex scenes.

Part 6, Mechanics: Foreshadowing your sexual language

So now we have some word ideas in mind. Maybe we've started thinking a bit more about what kind of hot-button (no pun intended) words we can use, what sort of tone we want to give our scenes? And how do we make sure that tone fits in with the rest of the book?

In some cases, your genre will assist you. I don't have to worry quite so much about this when I'm writing for Ellora's Cave simply because EC only publishes explicit, linguistically graphic sex. So if you're specifically writing erotic romance you have a bit more leeway (although having said that, I've been disappointed a few times by "erotic" romances that really were no more graphic than "regular" romances. In one case the only difference I could find was the use of the word "pussy" [a word I dislike, btw. I use it, because there aren't a lot of alternatives, but I avoid it whenever possible. There's just something about it—the hissy s, the stupid shape your mouth makes when you say it—that bugs me. I actually much prefer "cunt", but I know I'm weird in that respect. However, that brings up a very good point about reader tastes and expectations, which we will go into more at another time. I'm sure you know pretty much what I would say there anyway]. And believe me, just the word pussy does not eroticism make, at least not in my opinion.)

As we discussed in Part 4, your hero and heroine need to *react to* and *interact with* each other. This is where the work of writing the sex scene begins, and this is where you start making language choices that will determine what sort of scene you're going to write.

For example. Here is a snippet from the second chapter of *Blood Will Tell*, where Cecelia, already having noticed that Julian is sexy and attractive etc. etc., first has a real physical response to him:

Julian opened his mouth as if to speak, then shut it again. His gaze was making her nervous. Or was that nerves? It was more like…restless. Something in his eyes had changed as he looked at her, and without knowing why, her body suddenly ached for movement, her stomach filled with butterflies. Not to mention the distinct damp sensation in her pants as her pussy came to life under his dark scrutiny. She squirmed slightly, uncomfortably certain that he knew he was turning her on. Certain too that infuriating as he was, she wanted him. She never could resist a dare.

Here is the same moment—or the same type of moment anyway—from *Personal Demons* (this, by the way, is in Chapter Six—another important point):

Megan bit her lip and laid her fingertip on one of the little spikes. It was as dull as it looked. Without realizing it, she'd been expecting the spikes to feel slimy, alien. They did not. They felt like skin, no different from hers than anyone else's. Goosebumps appeared on his back. She ignored them. Ignored, too, the way her heartbeat quickened as she ran her fingertip all the way up his spine and back down. She repeated the motion with her palm. His skin was soft. The firm muscles beneath it seemed to ripple as she touched them. Heat gathered between her legs. Drawing in a long, shaky breath, Megan forced herself back to earth. This was not a seduction. The very idea was laughable—to her, at least. She had no doubt Greyson would be willing. She suspected Greyson would somehow manage to put off the apocalypse if doing so would get him laid.

So here we see something of the difference. In *Blood Will Tell*, we're thinking about sex less than two full chapters in—actually, she's already thought of it a few times, I believe the first mention is on page four—and we're thinking of it in graphic terms. Fun things are starting to happen in Cecelia's *pussy*; whereas Megan feels hot *between her legs*.

There's a few other differences as well, can you spot them? Cecelia is aching and squirming; she wants Julian and isn't afraid to admit it to herself. Megan is more conflicted. She's admitted earlier that she finds Greyson attractive but isn't willing to make the final step into saying she wants him; she's too guarded, and is convinced Greyson is simply a man-whore.

Now part of this is the women's characters. But part of it is deliberate choices to let the reader know what's coming. Someone finding Cecelia's pussy in chapter two (yes, I know, just giggle and move on) knows that we will probably get to the sex fairly soon—male and female funparts are like guns; you shouldn't take them out if you don't intend to use them—and that it will be linguistically at least somewhat frank. Whereas the reader who's made it to Chapter Six of Personal Demons knows that while there probably will be sex—even calling it "between her legs", I have still metaphorically flashed Megan's ladyparts at the readers—the language will probably not be as graphic.

This spreads to your whole book. The example I used previously was if the worst word in the book is "ass", you can't suddenly start throwing cunts and tits etc. around. Nor can you have two characters who have hot and graphic conversations or thoughts suddenly clam up or become flowery when it comes to actual sex. You need to keep the sexual tone consistent, right from the beginning (again, there are some exceptions; if your book is about a character's sexual awakening you can get away with this sort of modest-to-open change, but in general, you can't).

When your characters react to/interact with each other, their sexual thoughts and feelings must foreshadow the sex to come. If you use "pussy" (or whatever word) that first time, feel free to use it again; but if you never use it and suddenly do, your readers will be jarred by it, and the scene won't work as well as it should.

It just doesn't feel right, because whether you're in first person or third the fact is that a narrator who thinks/says "Gosh golly" when she's mad isn't likely to become Annie Sprinkle when it's time for sex. That doesn't mean you can't have fun with that sort of incongruity; you can, and to great effect (although I can't help but think that would probably be a more humorous than erotic scene).

But *your sex scene should not jar the reader*; you're trying to pull them in, to make them feel what the characters are feeling, and you can't do that if your language choices are throwing them out.

I've got a tad bit of space left in this post (I'm trying to keep them at around 1500 words each) so this seems like a good place to slip in discussion about terms for bodily fluids.

My personal feelings are as follows: I dislike any phrase that begins with the name of the body part from which the fluid in question emerges. "Pussy/cunt cream" or "Cock cream"...ech. No thank you. I find them distasteful. Likewise jokey terms like "baby batter" (who thought that was sexy, seriously?) I'm not crazy about "cum" either as a noun or as a verb—it reminds me too much of ads in the back of Hustler magazine, with some empty-eyed barely-legal being triple-teamed and the words "I'll make you cum" or something equally tacky above it. I don't have a problem with "come"; I just don't like the misspelling (frankly, any deliberate misspelling feels tacky to me). (Oh, and btw. In most erotic works "cum" is the noun; "come" is the verb:

"I'm going to come!" shouted Hero, and his cum spilled from him.)

So here's what I use:

For women:

Arousal cream fluids wetness "evidence/proof of her arousal/pleasure/orgasm." I've seen "honey" used, and like it fine, but I've not used it myself.

For men:

I have occasionally used "fluid"—for example, when describing pre-ejaculate—but generally I use "seed." It has a touch of old-world feeling I like. It's concise. It doesn't make me feel like I need to wash my hands afterward.

Of course, these are simply my preferences. But this is, I believe, another slightly touchy area (much like cunt. No pun intended). Just as "cunt" can get you in trouble, so too can too-explicit descriptions of semen or too much graphic accuracy. Perhaps because pornography is so focused on getting that Money Shot? So that just "feels" porny, and thus turns some women off? Hmm. That's a really interesting question, actually, but I digress. The point is, this is one area where I am very conservative because I feel it has the potential to really turn readers off. You are of course free to disagree and use whatever terms you like, but I personally would only go into ejaculatory details if the scene—and the other scenes in the book—were particularly graphic.

And really, I don't have a problem having only one word to describe semen (I think I might have used "semen" once or twice, now that I think of it). Because I just don't need to describe it very often. Even romance heroes don't usually come more than once per session, after all, and I don't need to describe the semen or explicitly mention it every time—that would be rather redundant.

So. Your assignment now is to (pick whichever applies):

Go back in your WIP and see what words you use when describing your characters's physical reactions to each other. Is that the level of terminology you want in your sex scene? Try heating it up by adding some more explicit words, and see what difference it makes, or lowering it down. Do that in the sex scene as well, using the word list I provided and/or your own words that you wrote down or thought of. See how the scene changes, and whether it blends into the rest of the book better or worse than before. Write a scene out of the blue, one either considerably more graphic than you're used to or considerably less. How does that feel? Comfortable? Uncomfortable?

Part 7, Mechanics: Odds and Ends about Language

(Note: All of these topics will be covered more throughout—well, except adverbs. This is just a bit of a language-specific overview.)

A while ago I saw a piece of writing advice concerning adverbs and sex scenes that I didn't really agree with. The advice was to use as many adverbs as you like, that a sex scene was one place where you don't need to look for other words or be careful about their use (and no, I don't think you should never ever use adverbs, but you do want to be careful. Why? Because adverbs are telling, nine times out of ten. Anyway.)

No, you shouldn't pepper your sex scene liberally with adverbs and pull every purple word you own out of the box. But you may find yourself using adverbs in sex scenes more often than in regular prose, and that's okay.

There are, quite simply, some words that need modification in a sex scene. When you say the hero pinches or rolls the heroine's nipples, the reader can be imagining all sorts of things—the kinds of things that may pull them out of the scene—unless you add that "gently." Or you may need to add "tenderly" to a look or a touch. Someone's eyes may close involuntarily; someone might suck greedily; or—one of my favorites, I admit—someone might do something *desperately*.

Not to mention, you may have already used all the straight action verbs you have, and so need to resort to modifying less intense verbs. You also might find that an adverb fits the rhythm of your scene. Rhythm is very important in sex (heh heh) and so it's very important when writing a sex scene. I think rhythm is one of those things that can't really be taught—you pick it up as you go—but to fill that rhythm out, to make your sentences flow, sometimes you need longer words. The point is, use whatever word you need, but don't feel like you have to modify every noun or verb, because you don't. You'll feel when you get it right, if not in the actual writing, than in the editing.

Now. Just as there are specific words for body parts, and hot-button words to evoke reactions, so there are words we use specifically for action. Some of them are on the hot-button list, some aren't. But one thing you're doing with those words is capturing a specific mood, whether it's romantic or passionate (not that you can't have both together of course) or angry or whatever. For example, if your characters are having a huge argument that explodes into passion—as Gruffydd and Isabelle do in my non-erotic medieval romance Black Dragon—you wouldn't use words like "eased" or adverbs like "gently". Instead you have something like this (I'm editing some stuff out so it may read a bit choppy—just focus on the active verbs here. We're going to look at part of this scene again later):

But he pulled her closer, making escape from the heat of his skin and the strength of his hands impossible…his mouth fell on hers, devouring her lips as his grip threatened to squeeze the life from her body. Instantly she was alight with desire, her breath coming in gasps as she clutched him.

His body was hot and slick with sweat and it felt better than anything she had ever experienced as she ran her hands feverishly across the hard muscles of his back and twisted his hair between her fingers.

With a growl, he swung her around and together they tumbled onto the thin straw mat. His hands ran up her legs, pushing the fabric of her dress up to her waist, caressing her thighs and delving into the most secret parts of her body. She writhed against his questing fingers.

She was faint; the air seemed to have left her lungs as she yanked at the cords that held up his clothing. He swatted her clumsy hands out of the way and undid them himself, his lips hot and demanding as he freed his turgid cock and drove it into her without elegance, his hands gripping her hips as if his life depended on keeping her steady for him.

Again and again he pounded into her while his fingers dug into her skin and her legs wrapped around his waist and squeezed. Their eyes locked, held, the anger on their faces turning into feverish need without losing intensity. Again they kissed, their mouths wrestling for dominance.

He bit her throat, her shoulders, holding her in place while she bucked and moaned beneath him. He punished her with his body and she retaliated with hers and he had no idea which of them would win or if there was even victory to be had as they battled with each other, locked together in terrible pleasure on the mat.

He felt her start to lose control, but did not let up his feverish pace. His ears were filled with the roaring of his blood. Dimly he heard her screaming his name, felt the exquisite pain of her fingernails slicing into his back as she arched herself almost off the mat, her body throbbing around his. And then he exploded, his body shaking with madness and ecstasy and he threw his head back and howled his pain and pleasure into the air, knowing that he was lost.

So, just like in a regular action scene, we're using very active words: *writhed, gripping, roaring, yanked, bucked, punished, battled*.

Now let's look at a romantic scene from the same book (again, edited so we can focus on language):

His tongue was a weapon of pleasure in her mouth as she spread her legs to accommodate him, already desperate to feel their bodies become one. She cradled his body over hers, his lean hips between her thighs. The hair on his legs was both strange and familiar to her, the scent of his skin overwhelming. She could drown in him, sink into him, and she lifted her hips, encouraging him to take her. To make their union complete.

He slid into her, agonizingly slowly so she could feel every inch of him. Her muscles tightened, gripping him, urging him deeper. He lifted his hands to the sides of her face, gently forcing her to look him in the eyes, forcing her to give him this last piece of herself. She did, and was rewarded with his secrets, with his soul. There would be no more hiding between them, not any more.

The movements of his body grew more urgent. He swelled inside her, stretching her walls, the heat and friction of their bodies together building to heights she'd never experienced before. The play of his muscles beneath her hands was precious, beautiful. The look in his eyes was even more so. She wrapped her legs around his thighs, moving with him, their breaths mingling.

His right hand found her left and clasped it, pressing it into the soft whiteness of the bed, their fingers interlocked as their bodies entwined. He spoke softly, words of love in French and Welsh, his voice adding another layer of sweetness to what was already perfect, and as they moved together and neared the pinnacle of pleasure, he claimed her mouth again in a final searing kiss.

She exploded beneath him, her body arching upwards, her free hand clutching at his back, pulling his hair, her legs squeezing him as she gasped his name, barely hearing hers on his lips as they both burst apart with terrifying, glorious intensity. He was hers and that was all that mattered now.

Now, that's not my favorite sex scene I've ever written, and it's not particularly explicit, but do you see the differences? The rhythm itself is different; the second scene uses more flowing sentences, more commas, instead of the breathlessness of the first. And we're still using some of the same words, but the feeling isn't at all the same. We have Gruffydd "gently forcing" her to look into his eyes. In the first scene he *drove* himself into her; in this one he *slides*, slowly. She *encourages* him; she *urges* him deeper. They *clasp* hands. She *drowns* in him (although be careful of water imagery as it can be very cliché; we're going to do that later too.)

(There's another big difference between those two scenes, and it will be the subject of its own post at some point in the next two weeks. Does anyone know what it is? [It's not the POV switch, although we'll do that too.])

So apologies for this segment being a little weaker than the others. But I think it's a good overview, some things to keep in mind as we move on. Rhythm, for example, probably won't get its own post as it's both too intrinsic and not complex enough for a long discussion. But now that you have examples in front of you it's something you can keep in mind and look for in later posts and in your own work.

So that's your little weekend exercises for those who are playing along. You can do all or none or a combination: Write two sex scenes using the same basic action words, but varying the rhythm and length of the sentences. See how that changes the mood. Take one of your current scenes. Combine two sentences into one throughout. Or divide longer sentences. See what that does. Replace action verbs with basic verbs and adverbs. Is that stronger or weaker?

Part 8, Mechanics: Illustrating/Advancing Relationship

The following are two snippets from sex scenes in my EC release *Accustomed to His Fangs*, a vampire *My Fair Lady* spoof. I chose an unpublished work (*unpublished at the time of writing this) so everyone gets to play along.

One is from the beginning of the story. One is from the end. You tell me which:

She reached for him, longing to feel that skin under her fingertips again, and he leaned forward to allow it. His cock touched her thigh, its hard thickness hot enough to scorch her skin. An answering heat flowed through her body, although she thought she might not be ready to take that length inside her after what she'd just experienced.

She was wrong. In one swift movement, Sebastian leaned forward, cupping her face in one hand and using the other to guide himself into her body, impaling her, stretching her as he drove himself balls-deep into her slick heat.

"Vadushkia," he whispered. A shiver ran through his body and transferred itself to her as he started moving, slow, steady thrusts that built the pressure in her body again.

Her exhaustion left her. Her hands wandered over his strong back, down the heavy muscles of his arms that shook as he kept up his rhythm. His lips found hers, more tenderly than before. As if a circuit had been completed with his kiss, Becky felt his pleasure run through her in a rush, felt it leave and go back to him, only to come back. Again she left her body and found herself in his. Again she was back in hers with him. If she'd thought she was floating before, when his masterful tongue coaxed multiple orgasms from her trembling frame, she knew it now. This was unreal, unbelievable and she prayed it wouldn't stop.

***

Her hand stole down his stomach to his cock, squeezing him, pulling him forward. The need to be inside her overwhelmed him and sweat broke out on his skin as he pressed her back further into the pale silk sheets. Around them, candles flickered and wavered. The whispers of his ancestors, of the Gods of the *rotagosja*, echoed in his ears. His muscles screamed, tightening as he fought to accept her change for her. He positioned himself at her entrance and slid inside.

She was so tight, so wet. He squeezed his eyes shut as her muscles squeezed his cock. Her back arched, pressing her breasts up to his chest, exposing her throat. Her canines were already lengthening. The sight excited him more than he'd ever dreamed.

"Rebecca," he whispered, driving himself deeper into her. She responded with a moan and wrapped her legs around his waist, rocking her hips up toward him. Even her body felt different, warmer, more alive. The scent of her skin, that perfect Rebecca-scent that always made something inside him feel both cheerful and feral at the same time, had changed. It did not lessen his reaction. Instead it called to that feral part, called to the barely tamed wildness of his race, and let him know she was one of them.

The ache in his body, the burning of his bones as he carried her pain, started to lessen. The transition had almost ended. His muscles shook as tension grew in his pelvis, in his stomach. For the first time, he thought of the chance that their love could create a new life. The idea sent his hips thrusting faster, harder, as the woman he loved matched his every move with delirious speed.

Ha! I can hear you now: "No fair! It's obvious which one is from later in the story!"

And my response to that is...Damn right. *It should be.*

Now, in an erotic romance, there are a lot of sex scenes. It's possible to take a snippet from a scene near the beginning, and trade it with a snippet near the end, and perhaps find them interchangeable. But that's a snippet. Not a whole scene.

Remember, if the sex isn't advancing story, character, or relationship, it shouldn't be there. Which means something should be different between the characters in every scene, no matter how small. Even if it's simply something about the new ease they've found, or how he nibbled her neck in the spot her knew she loved, or something. (Ideally it should be more, but it also depends on what the scene is most heavily focused on.)

So let's look at these two snippets—and a little more at Part Seven's *Black Dragon* snippets, as well. Remember how I mentioned the one other big difference between those two *Dragon* scenes?

The difference was, in the first scene, the two are fighting—it's literally sex as a weapon, and they're using sex as a substitute for emotion. In the second, sex is an adjunct to their emotion. Rather than Gruffydd taking Isabelle, they're taking each other—Isabelle is a more active participant in this scene, or rather, her actions are described more specifically, which makes her seem more active. Their movements are slower—they're taking their time, looking at each other, being with each other.

We have the same with the two *Accustomed* scenes. Yes, there's the obvious stuff—Becky's change, Sebastian thinking about babies (he's such a sap), the candles and ancestors which indicate this is no ordinary sex scene.

But in the first the focus is on Becky's sensations. There is—or at least I hope there is—a feeling of discovery in Becky's hoping it doesn't stop. There's a sense of impersonal-ness (is that a word?) in the first scene. Becky knows it's Sebastian with her, she's thinking of him by name, but she's not making love with him. All he is to her in that scene is broad shoulders, a talented mouth, a hard cock. She's not looking into his eyes, or really at him at all. She's not wondering what he's thinking or feeling, beyond the physical. She is totally focused on herself.

In the second we have more of a sense of people doing this together. Sebastian isn't just thinking of himself, and neither—in the bits from her POV—is Becky. It isn't simply a matter of moving more slowly or being more tender, because that isn't always the case. It's a lot of little things: focus on the other person, need for them and not just their various body parts, thoughts and feelings. It's the difference between Hero wanting to be inside Heroine's *hot cunt*, or wanting to be inside *her*.

Now, not every scene is going to be quite as obvious as the snippets above. For example, the bathroom scene in *Blood Will Tell* or the up-against-the-lightpost scene in *Eighth Wand* are both pretty violent, really. But the reasoning behind them and what they're meant to show are different as well—both are more story-advancing than character-advancing, although they of course do their share of both. The reckless passion of the bathroom scene, for example, stems directly from Julian's frustration at being unable to tell Cecelia how he feels and from his sense of having failed her. This is obvious from the dialogue and his thoughts before the scene, and through his thoughts during about seeking redemption, trying to forget, etc.

Everything counts. What your characters are thinking while they're having sex is at least as important as what they're doing, and you can show the way their relationship advances simply by changing their focus, or the course of their thoughts, just as much as you can add a little staring-into-each-others'-eyes or sweet dialogue. It all adds up to give the reader a much more complete picture of these people an their relationship.

44

(Oh, and conversely, you can use this change in focus to show a sexual relationship that isn't going anywhere. If your characters never think of each other, or think of each other only in the most base physical terms, you're subtly signaling the reader that this is a relationship without a future, no matter how pleasurable or hot the sex may be.)

So. Here's an assignment. Grab any book (with sex in it!) from your shelf. Read the sex scene, but focus on how much the characters think of each other, and what they think. What does that tell you about their relationship? Now look at one of your own scenes. Have you used the POV character's thoughts and what they see and feel to illustrate their feelings?

Try writing some new scenes, from the viewpoint of a character totally in love. Now try one with a couple who's been having some problems, and is having sex more out of duty than anything else. It can still be good sex, but how does it change the course of their thoughts? Are they able to lose themselves in the physical as easily?

Part 9, Character: Who's on top?

Of course, who's on top isn't the only way to illustrate character through your sex scenes. It's just one of the most obvious, one of the easiest to use. And honestly, it's one of very few "writer's tricks" that work, that are there for a real reason, and never become cliché. *Somebody* has to be on top, after all—at least some of the time, heh heh—so you have a distinct advantage there.

I don't only mean who's on top in the literal physical sense, either. I mean who initiates, who takes charge? Who's doing the seducing, who's making the other work for it, who wants who more? (Yes, I know that second "who" should be "whom." I just don't care.)

I don't think I've made any real secret of my preference for dominant men in romance, and those men do tend to be in the driver's seat, so to speak—at least on the surface. But while it's easy to look at the man making all the moves and see him as the one in charge, to me it's a lot subtler than that; he's the one brave enough to put himself out there; he's the one taking the risk and admitting he has, if not feelings, physical desires, yes. But the woman is in charge. *She's* the one who says yes or no.

But it's for just that reason that when the woman takes charge it can really deepen the relationship, the conflict, and the story.

For me, the moment when the woman takes charge, even if it's as simple as being on top, is the moment the relationship makes a subtle change. In *Blood Will Tell* Cecelia walked directly into a planned seduction; she was prey, plain and simple, for Julian—a man who knew how to seduce and was used to being in control. But when, two days later, she takes the initiative, it's a signal, and she means it to be. She's going to be an active partner in this budding relationship; she's going to show him what she's made of. And by doing that she moves herself even further out of the "position" Julian originally placed her in.

Likewise, Aleeza in *Demon's Triad* is the active seducer with her first partner, Dorand. Not so with Ferrin, who is much more of a sexual threat to her. He's the seducer from the start; it isn't until she realizes she has deep feelings for him that she becomes aggressive—Dorand is more immediately trustworthy, so Aleeza doesn't feel the emotional vulnerability with him she feels with Ferrin.

As I said back in the "Do you need a sex scene post", everyone in the world who has sex does it in a slightly different way. Obviously not the direct physical act, but everything around it. A lot of this will be covered in foreplay later, and a lot of it involves dialogue which we'll do shortly. But the way your characters touch, when they look at each other and what they look at, what they're thinking, what they like—it's all different for everyone.

Here's an easy example. Do your characters look at each other? Do they look into each others's eyes? They don't have to; honestly, they shouldn't always, because that can be just as hackneyed and boring as any other stereotypically "romantic" moment. But for a character who hides? A character who doesn't reveal a lot about themselves? The moment when s/he finally locks gazes with their partner can be a big moment. You don't have to emphasize it in any particular way, you don't have to make it a Big Moment. But the reader will see it, and sense it, because we've all felt the difference it makes when we really look at our partners. (Did you know that young babies are awakened and stimulated by direct eye contact? The best way to rouse a sleepy baby is to look directly into its eyes. Really. Think about that for a minute, and how you can use it.)

What might be the response of someone who's always in control to having that control stripped from them in bed? What might be the response of someone who is always the submissive partner suddenly being the dominant one? Would s/he be scared, tentative? Triumphant? What about a woman who's always been very open about her needs in bed? How would she react to a man who clearly expected to be in the driver's seat?

What about a couple who laughs a lot, whose main form of communication is joking? What happens when they stop laughing? What are their favorite parts of each other's bodies, and how much attention do they pay to those parts (and I mean things like the small of her back, the curve of a shoulder, a scar on a chest, not the obvious)? How about a woman who is self-conscious about her body? Wouldn't she be a little more apt to try and hide bits of it or to avoid certain positions? Does the hero know or sense her feelings and go out of his way to reinforce them? Perhaps the hero is the self-conscious one. What does the heroine do?

Why is the one in control the one in control? Did the other person willingly give up control, or did they never take it? How does that coincide with what we already know about them, or does it?

In *As the Lady Wishes*, Anna J. Evans and I created Lila, a woman who'd been abused by her husband and had finally escaped from him and his iron rule. One of the first things she did was buy herself a vibrator—because her husband had found her normal needs and desires repugnant. The vibrator (and the junk food in her cabinets) was a symbol of independence to Lila, and a way to show she was going to live for herself for once.

But when Arthur, an ancient Druid who'd been imprisoned in a painting for thousands of years and forced to grant wishes when set free, seduces her (thus fulfilling her wish), Lila still insists he get some pleasure from the act as well. This not only sets Lila up as someone who is still a caring and giving person despite her horrific past, but gives Arthur a reason to see her as more than Yet Another Master. For me, despite the fact that this scene takes place twenty pages into the book (and we've already set up Lila's personality and past), the moment when she refuses to allow Arthur to have anything less than his own pleasure (yes, we're talking blowjobs here, folks) is the moment when Lila really becomes a fully rounded character, strong and even more likeable than she was before (and I really liked Lila). After everything she'd been through, after Arthur informs her he's there specifically for her pleasure, she still refuses to be solely The Taker.

My heroes—most romance or romantic heroes, really—tend to be pretty masterful when it comes to the old sexing. They know what they're doing, and they do it well. But to a man, they don't orgasm until the heroine has done so at least once. Why? Because they're not selfish in bed, and because they get pleasure from giving it to their partners. To me this is a huge character point. A man can be as selfish, snide, or tricky as he wants to be in life—let's take Greyson Dante as an example, as he never does anything without first figuring out what's in it for him—but it would be absolutely unthinkable to him to ignore Megan's needs in bed. More than that, he offers to wear a condom even though he knows and has explained how it's unnecessary. To me that was an important moment, and not just because that bit of dialogue enabled me to dispense with the stupid condoms (which I loathe writing, by the way. There is nothing sexy about condoms and all the damn she-put-the-condom-on-with-her-teeth scenes in the world will never convince me that there is).

It showed Megan, and more importantly the reader, several things: how very much he wanted Megan, how he understood she might not trust or believe him and accepted it, how he was willing to put himself out to set her mind at ease, the mere fact that he brought it up at all. What does this say about his character?

What does it say about a man's character if he isn't concerned about such things, and is it always that he's selfish? It might not be; maybe he was with a woman who told him not to bother. Maybe he was with a woman who faked it, and so is doing what he's always been told is mind-shatteringly faboo but leaves the heroine cold. How can you twist a situation like that and show the readers something really, deeply important about the character, not just that he's selfish and/or doesn't care?

The great thing about sex scenes is, they enable you to literally and figuratively strip your characters bare and see what happens. You get to examine them at their most open level, their most unconscious waking level. When we have sex we're not thinking as much; what we do is instinctive. It's a golden opportunity to give the reader some real insight into the character themselves, if they're selfish or giving, bored or carried away by passion, scared or triumphant or desperate or cold.

Your character's sex scenes should be a barometer of who and where they are; it's themselves at their most basic.

Here's a little assignment: again, look at some of your sex scenes. Do you see the characters as individuals in them? What do their actions tell you about themselves—not the relationship, but them themselves? Do they meet problems and fears head-on, and so make love the same way—boldly, and without looking back? Or are they more tentative, nervous? How does this reinforce their character development throughout the story?

Write a paragraph of *tell* about one character having sex. Like, "Jack has a very naturalistic approach to sex, and isn't ashamed of it. He loves women and everything about them. To him sex is like an amusement

50

park ride. He's very open about his needs and rarely lets them be ignored. He doesn't ignore his partner either, and he doesn't understand people who are shy in bed."

How would that character have sex? He'd probably take the heroine's hand and show her what to do. He'd probably try a lot of different things with her, and depending on what sort of woman she is, would be either thrilled with her openness or confused or even frustrated with her reticence. Maybe he would work to thaw her out a bit? Maybe he would go too far, or maybe not? Surely he'd watch her pretty closely to gauge her reactions, right?

Now read one of your scenes, or a scene from a book, or whatever, and write a paragraph of *tell* about those characters. What did the sex scene teach you about them?

Part 10, Character and Dialogue: Shut up and do it

I wasn't sure if the topic of dialogue really fits in character or relationship/story—and we'll be discussing it a lot more in Foreplay. But hey, we're merging the subjects a little bit anyway as we go, so why not, right?

Okay. I hate talky sex scenes. I really dislike them. As Miranda said on *Sex and the City*, sex is the one place where you don't have to talk. It just feels weird to have characters carrying on a conversation during sex (most of the time; yes, I can think of situations when the ability to carry on a normal-sounding conversation while otherwise engaged would come in handy, or whatever, but in general). I think there are far better things for mouths to be doing, and frankly, I just find it a little dull. Unsexy. Shut up and do it already.

That doesn't mean the act has to take place in hallowed silence. It's fine if your characters want to say each other's names, or the ever-popular "Yes! Yes!" or "Ohgodpleasedon'tstop" (which is totally sexy, IMO) or, if we're having one of those lovey-dovey moments, the "I love you"s and whatever. It's all fine. Sometimes it can work very well. There's also the ever-popular patented Alpha Male "Come for me," in which the heroine invariably does (any of you ladies out there want to say if that works in real life? Cuz I've never tried it, but I have my doubts).

But I cannot count the number of sex scenes I've read where the characters are having long conversations about how they feel, what they're doing, how much they like it, what they're going to do next, blah blah blah blah, and it is so uninteresting I want to fall asleep. Who does that? I have never been with a man who insists on constantly talking during sex (aside from the general babble, which I do like—you know, "words falling out of his mouth", but none of them detailed—I used this in *Personal Demons*, for example, because Greyson is such a talker most of the time anyway it made sense) and I don't think I would want to be. Doesn't he have more important things to focus on?

The trick is, keep it simple. Remember, these people are having sex. Supposedly really good, hot sex. How long a speech do you think you can make in the middle of the sort of sweaty, rampant, mind-blowing multiple-orgasm-playground sex our characters tend to have?

I know we play with the bounds of physical reality a bit. (How many grown men—above the age of, say, thirty—do you know who can go four or five times in one night, one right after another, without the aid of modern medicine? Yeah, I thought so.) So I guess it's not totally out of the question to believe people are capable of long eloquent speeches while performing semi-acrobatic sexual acts. But seriously, let's try and keep this to a decent level.

Because dialogue interrupts the sex scene, nine times out of ten. Or rather, too much dialogue does. Anything over a sentence or two is too much.

But what are your characters saying?

Here's what I think is the biggest issue, the most common pitfall in writing dialogue during sex: Writers forget characterization, and write what they think is sexy or romantic.

And it might be, sure. But when you've set up a strong, silent hero who doesn't talk about his feelings, it's simply not appropriate or believable to have him suddenly giving long, flowery speeches of love. And to be perfectly honest, while I've heard some lovey-dovey speeches in my time, and even made a few (please control your shock, I know), it's not usually been during actual sex. Why? Because that's just too much. Speech first, then sex. Or sex first, then speech. But—and here's today's little theme—in sex, our bodies talk much more eloquently than anything we can say.

Nor is it appropriate to go in the other direction, and make him a Pottymouth McGee. This is, I think, another common error: Thinking that "hot" dialogue will make the scene itself hotter. But it won't. Because honestly? Perhaps it's unenlightened of me or something, and I'm sure it's kind of amusing coming from me, Miss Dirty Language, but it feels disrespectful somehow to me. I don't mean in every situation; such language can be useful in dialogue at certain points in a story. I've written it before. And I've written a few scenes along the line of "Does that feel good? Tell me," etc. But I believe when we're talking about "normal" men and women, getting naked together for the first time, it's rude and vulgar for a character to force dirty talk on another character. There's a difference between "I'm going to fuck you now, Heroine," (hot) and "Here I am, fucking you. Feel me fucking you? Yes, you feel it. Because my big cock blah blah blah" and you just want to smack him and tell him to give it a rest.

In fact, in looking back on my collected works (ooh, I can't decide if that sounds pretentious or impressive) I've found only one sex scene with extensive dialogue, and it isn't technically a sex scene. It's *Eighth Wand*'s mutual masturbation scene, and even it stays, um, within my dialogue comfort zone, let's say. Here Royd and Prudence, brought together by magic and knowing that no matter how deeply and quickly they've fallen for each other a future is impossible, give each other something to remember later (edited for brevity):

"When I do this," he said into her neck, "when I do this at home, *uishta*, do you know what I'll be thinking of?"

She shook her head, still unable to stop watching. He ran his palm over the head, then swirled it back down, his fist tightening. "I'll think of this. This, now. You watching me."

Now she understood why he wanted this. Not just because he wanted to see her open herself in such an intimate fashion. But because he would be alone again, alone and thinking of her.

"I'll think of your body," he continued. "How it feels to be buried inside you. How you look at me, the sound of your voice. The scent of your skin. The taste of you."

Again she reached for him. This time he let go of himself and took her hand, guiding it to her pussy. She bit her lip. "Royd, I—"

"Show me. Give me something more to picture in my mind, something to imagine you doing. Let me pretend we're doing it at the same time. Please…"

She hesitated, aware that beyond everything else they'd done together, this was totally uncharted territory. Aware it was something she could give him that would be his alone. Her thighs parted. […]

"You have no idea how beautiful you look," he whispered. "How beautiful you are, to me." The words made her bold. She rolled over him to his other side, suddenly determined that if he wanted a memory, if he wanted to picture her pleasuring herself, she would give him something to picture.

Her head rested on the pillows. She spread her legs wider, aware that this was turning her on in more ways than one. The blackness in his eyes was almost frightening, the naked desire on his face intoxicating. His hand moved faster as she started moving faster too, dipping her fingertips into her cunt and bringing them back out coated with her juices. Every bit of skin between her legs was over-sensitized and needy, and everywhere she touched brought a different sensation, a different shock of pleasure. She slid her fingertip around her entrance, then just inside, then around again, spreading her legs as wide as they would go. She slid her left hand down too, to hold her lips apart.

"Yes, Prudence," Royd gasped. "Show me everything."

Without planning to, she started talking. "I wish this was your hand," she whispered. "Your fingers slipping into me. It's so hot in there, Royd, so hot and so wet. Can you see how wet I am?"

"Yes," he groaned. "Yes."

"That's because of you. Because I'm thinking of you, thinking about your tongue and your fingers and your cock...I want you so bad."

Now I'm rather proud of that particular bit of dirty talk, because, just as it was for Prudence, it wasn't planned for me either. But I think the most important thing about this scene—aside from the fact that along with being (hopefully) pretty hot, it strikes me as rather sad—is that the dialogue spurs the action. Royd's verbal, vocal approval makes Prudence bold. When she finally begins to speak, it's from a place she's never touched within herself (and I don't mean physically).

In other words, this isn't dialogue for dialogue's sake; it's dialogue that expands character and relationship, and moves the scene itself forward. It seems to me—it's the "make it hot hot hotter" thing again—some writers forget that dialogue doesn't simply exist to heat things up. It has to be in character. It has to be the impetus for the movements; either the mouth or the body must talk. Because Pru and Royd aren't technically touching each other or having sex here, I felt free to let them say a lot more. Quite simply, they had no other way to communicate. But in an effective sex scene—one involving actual intercourse—there should be lots of other ways.

Also, you may notice the dialogue tags here stray from my semi-loose "always use 'said'" edict. I think you do have a bit more play in this in a sex scene. Don't go overboard; but "said" can be a little matter-of-fact for a sex scene.

Like I said, dialogue is an important part of foreplay, and we'll be getting much more deeply into all the fun that can be had with talking before. We may even have a chance to get into talk after, too. But remember, what your characters say and how they say it has to serve their characters, not just the scene. In fact, I believe it should serve their characters more than the scene.

You don't need dialogue to make a sex scene hot, but you do need the characters to be true to themselves. Talky sex is telling, not showing, the majority of the time.

If they're not in character, the reader will see it, and it will pull them out of the scene. Sex isn't the time to get fancy with dialogue.

If your characters have that much to say to each other, write a dialogue scene, not a sex scene. The point of a sex scene is to let their bodies do the talking.

Some exercises to try: Reread one of your sex scenes. Remove all the dialogue and read it again. Does it flow better, or does it really need the dialogue? Add the dialogue back in, one line at a time.

If your scene has no dialogue, add some in. How does that change the scene?

Find some published sex scenes you really like. How much dialogue is in there? How do you think that dialogue adds to the heat of the scene? Would it be hotter without it, or would it not flow as well? Remember, this is all about rhythm.

Write a scene where the characters constantly talk about what they're doing. How does that work for you?

Remember, *this is all my opinion*. The exercises are designed (and I use that word loosely, ha) to make you think about how *you* use these elements and whether or not you agree.

Part 11: Telling Isn't Sexy

Q. What is a sex scene about?
A. A sex scene is about sex.

Except it isn't. Or rather, it is about the physical act of sex only at its most basic level. Sex is the action, but just as our action scenes are about more than that (danger, adventure, knowledge gained, change, whatever) so are our sex scenes.

A sex scene is about what your characters are feeling, thinking, and learning about themselves and each other.

And this is the key to writing a hot sex scene. Let's take a look at this scene from *Blood Will Tell* with all of the physical sensation, thinking, and emotion removed—as well as all the foreplay, because foreplay is *hugely* important and will be covered extensively later. In other words, it is straight sex, just physical action:

Without preamble he slammed into her hilt-deep. Cecelia's back arched and she cried out. Her voice mingled with his as he too yelled. Gripping her hips hard, he pulled back, then thrust again, and again.

He reached down between her legs, finding her clit and rubbing it. He pinched it lightly, tugging on it, then letting go and grazing it in a circular motion with his palm. Her cries grew louder. So did his. His free hand braced the top of her ass, and he shifted so he could slip his thumb into the puckered entrance and fuck her with it that way, continuing his assault on her clit.

She came. "Julian!"

He smacked her ass. His handprint showed red on one soft, round cheek as blood rushed to the surface.

"Cecelia," he groaned, "Fuck…Cecelia…I could fuck you a million times and it wouldn't be enough. It's never enough."

She didn't reply. He pulled out and flipped her around, propping her up on the counter. Her legs closed around his waist. Glasses and jars flew to the floor as he swept them away with his free hand. Her arms were back, bracing herself on the counter, her legs open.

He changed his pace, rolling his hips with every thrust. He leaned forward to kiss her, raising one hand to squeeze her breast and tug at her nipple.

Her head fell back, exposing her throat. He pulled her closer, tangling his fingers into her hair to yank her head to the side. He came. His cock jerked deep inside her. He felt her burst apart around him, her fluids joining his. Her fingernails dug into his back, breaking the skin. He fisted his hand in her hair and lowered his face to her throat, his fangs tearing through her skin. It sent him back into a second orgasm.

Now let's see the same scene as it was published:

Without preamble he slammed into her hilt-deep. The beast within him, the vampire who craved her blood, roared with delight as Cecelia's back arched and she cried out. Her voice mingled with his as he too yelled, a wordless cry of triumph. Gripping her hips so hard his fingers hurt, he pulled back, then thrust again, and again, watching himself slide into and out of her, watching her skin grip his.

The scent of her arousal hung heavy in the air like some exotic, expensive perfume, driving his sexual fury even higher. A glance in the bathroom mirror showed him Cecelia's face transported by pleasure, her eyes closed, her mouth open as she cried out again and again in time with his thrusts.

The folds and fissures of her cunt massaged him, provided delicious friction against him as he ruthlessly stretched them, bruised them, forced them—and her—to comply to his demands. He reached down between her legs,

59

finding her hard little clit and rubbing it, feeling it stiffen further. He pinched it lightly, tugging on it, then letting go and grazing it in a circular motion with his palm.

Her cries grew louder. So did his.

His free hand braced the top of her ass, and he shifted so he could slip his thumb into the puckered entrance and fuck her with it that way, filling her cunt with his cock and her ass with his thumb, continuing his assault on her clit with fingers soaking from her juices. Her cunt swelled and tightened around him as she came, shaking, screaming, a flood of hot liquid pouring from her to drench his cock. "Julian!"

He almost fell apart, but stopped himself just in time, holding himself back. Instead he smacked her ass, hard enough to feel the vibrations deep inside her.

His handprint showed red on one soft, round cheek as blood rushed to the surface. It took every ounce of strength he had not to turn completely feral at the sight.

"Cecelia," he groaned, "Fuck…Cecelia…I could fuck you a million times and it wouldn't be enough. It's never enough."

She didn't reply, but her cunt still spasming around him told him everything.

He pulled out and flipped her around, propping her up on the counter. Her legs closed around his waist, pulling him close so he could sink back into her. Glasses and jars flew to the floor as he swept them away with his free hand, heedless of the sound they made hitting the tiles.

He let her slide a little farther back, resting her more securely on the cold tile so he could thrust into her with more force. The fever raging in his body still gripped him, gripped them both.

Her arms were back, bracing herself on the counter, her legs open so he could watch their bodies joining. Her pussy gleamed, her dewy lips plump and pink above his thrusting cock, so engorged it looked almost purple. Filled with blood.

He groaned and closed his eyes, then squeezed her waist, pressing her closer to him, urging her to put her arms around his neck and hold on. This she did, her breasts bobbing against his chest with every movement. He changed his pace, feeling himself getting ready to come apart, rolling his hips with every thrust.

Heat poured into his pelvis, building to an unbearable level. Every muscle in his body vibrated and tightened as he leaned forward to kiss her, raising one hand to squeeze her breast and tug at her nipple. Her mouth tasted sweet, and he savored it, savored the connection with the last bit of sanity he had left.

Her head fell back, exposing her throat. The beast in him roared, shook, all but flew from his body in eager, blinding need. He pulled her closer, tangling his fingers into her hair to yank her head to the side, keeping her gaze from him or the mirror.

He came. His body vibrated, trembling with a force like he'd never before experienced. His cock jerked deep inside her, sending waves of unbelievable pleasure through him. He felt her burst apart around him, her fluids joining his. Her fingernails dug into his back, breaking the skin, sending exquisite pain shooting through his body.

His hoarse, low shout turned into something even deeper, something that rumbled in his throat as his vision went red. Now. *Now! NOW!*

He fisted his hand in her hair and lowered his face to her throat, his fangs tearing through her skin, slipping into her mind with ease and tasting her passion and pleasure along with her blood.

It was enough to send him back into a second orgasm, something he'd only experienced once or twice in his life. He spun on a thread, barely attached to his body, riding huge endless waves of pure pleasure, sending webs out through her to share it with him.

Now, if I've done my job properly, the second example should be MUCH more stimulating, erotically and otherwise. In the first all we get are bodies; in the second we have the addition of emotion, feeling, thought, sensation, personality... in other words, the first shows us nothing (or very little) about the characters, while the second gives us at least some insight into them. (Again,

61

the majority of this takes place during foreplay.) The first is just bodies; the second is people. The first is telling; the second shows. If we can't feel what your characters feel, we're not feeling anything at all.

This is the difference between amateurish porn and erotica or erotic romance; porn is about bodies, erotica is about people. Telling isn't sexy; it's pornography, and it's not what we're doing.

We'll be covering this in greater depth with more examples throughout; this is simply the first shot across the bow, as it were.

Today's exercise: Read a couple of published sex scenes you find particularly arousing. How much of those scenes is pure physical description? How much is emotion, feeling, thinking? Which do you think is more important, what ratio is the most satisfying to you?

Now read one of your own scenes. Have you used emotion, sensation, and thought as effectively as you might, or do you think you can improve? Remember, every scene is different; some will call for more emotion/sensation/thought, some less, but it must be there if the scene is going to work.

Write a sex scene with no physical description at all. Just your character's thoughts, emotions, and feelings. Now add the physical stuff in, bit by bit, until you've reached the "ratio" that pleases you the most (this will probably be different with every scene, btw.) How does that feel to you? Do you feel more or less confident about that scene than about the others you've written?

Part 12: How graphic do you need to go?

Not very. Really. Obviously I think the more graphic the better, but... As we saw in the last post, the key to a hot sex scene isn't so much what the characters are doing. It's what they're feeling. I'm going to share with you a scene from a book I didn't write. This is from Sharon Kay Penman's (http://www.sharonkaypenman.com) second medieval mystery, and a fantastic book—I've blogged before about how much I love her work and how I think the hero of the mysteries, Justin de Quincy, is hot as hell. Funnily enough, this book is the first of the Justin books I read, and it's this scene which took him from attractive and appealing to totally, completely HOT for me. This is from *Cruel As the Grave,* used with permission:

The lovemaking that followed was unlike anything Justin had experienced before. There was more than lust in their eager, out-of-control coupling. He'd brought anger into the bed, too, a stifled rage that found expression now in the urgency of his demands. He was not gentle, not tender, afire with his need for release, for redemption, for oblivion.

Claudine was soon caught up in his incendiary passion, burning with the same frenzied fever, and for a brief time, there were no secrets between them, no betrayals, nothing but sweat and scratches and muffled cries and pleasure so intense it was almost akin to pain.

When it was over, Justin was exhausted, drenched in perspiration, and shaken, both by the reckless abandon of their lovemaking and that it had happened at all.

See? Now look at that scene again. There is not one graphic word or line in it; no erections, no cocks, no pussies or "entrances" or "tunnels" or anything of the sort. There's not even an "he entered her" or "he shoved himself inside her." The most graphic words in it, in fact, are "lovemaking" and "coupling."

But it's still hot. It's still a satisfying scene. I would have liked it to be more graphic, sure, because of my freakishly obsessive love for Justin. But this was fine with me, especially as Cruel as the Grave is not a romance; it's a mystery. While the Justin/Claudine relationship is an important subplot, I don't expect the same level of explicitness from other genres; while I expect the sex scene in a romance or erotic romance and, to a lesser degree, urban fantasy, to be arousing, I don't expect the same from other genres (although obviously I'm happiest if they are).

When this scene is done, even though it's only one paragraph plus a few sentences long, we feel like we have read an entire sex scene. By amping up the language as she goes (see how the first few sentences are matter-of-fact statements, and as the scene goes on we see more commas, more words upon words, until finally we have the last phrase of the actual scene, with no commas at all, so the sentence is read in one breathless gulp) Penman makes us see the scene. We *see* candlelight flickering off those bodies; we hear the sounds they make; we see the sheets crumple and twist beneath them.

And most importantly, we see the depth of Justin's feelings, which you guys don't know about, because you haven't read the book (which is why you need to go buy it *right now*; well, first buy the first book *The Queen's Man*, then this one. Buy them together so you can go right from one to the other).

But I bet all of you can give an educated guess as to why Justin is so angry in this scene, and what went wrong between him and Claudine.

Now, again, if I've done my job, the frenzied lust in this scene and the frenzied lust in last segment's *Blood Will Tell* scene are on a par with each other—by which I mean you felt it in both scenes. But my scene is extremely graphic, and this one isn't, and that's why I chose both of these as examples.

How graphic the language is, is entirely up to you. Obviously I am a fan of the graphic scene, because I have a dirty mind. You may not like it or be comfortable with it, and in those cases, this is perhaps the type of scene you could be going for (and, again, FOREPLAY. Very important. You can get away with only a few lines of actual sex if you've done a good job with foreplay. But I'm getting ahead of myself now.)

I got a question that made me realize I'd forgotten something important when we discussed language, so this seems like a good place to fit it in. The question related to finding appropriate language for the audience and scene, and the use of graphic terms in romantic scenes. Here's what I do. The more romantic the scene, the more euphemistic the language.

I don't mean I start pulling out the purple prose, just that words like "cunt", which I'm perfectly comfortable tossing around in other scenes, do not feel to me as if they belong in a very romantic scene—a "consummation" scene, as opposed to a sex scene. In my romances there is almost always a "we love each other" sex scene, when all questions have been answered and our characters have admitted their feelings and, naturally, the intensity of their feelings makes them want to physically express them. So they do.

I never use "cunt" in those scenes. In fact, I rarely use any graphic language at all (cock is still in there, of course, because as we all know, cock is always appropriate and is always welcome, like French fries or a cold drink. Cock is the anti-drug. I could come up with these all day, people, seriously).

But beyond that, those scenes are heavily emotional. They should still be arousing, but think about it. When you had sex with your partner, or your past partner, or whatever, for the first time when you knew you were really in love, were you competing in the Kama Sutra Olympics or were you really, deeply, feeling instead of acting? (If you care to answer that anonymously [or as yourself, of course], btw, I'd be very interested in the replies, to see if I'm right about that or not).

That doesn't mean those scenes can't be wild, if that's the sort of couple you're writing. It just means that those scenes must above all focus on sex as the culmination of and expression of love. It can still be arousing, it can still be hot, it can be however you want it to be—but I personally believe graphic language of the highest level doesn't belong in those scenes, because it spoils the mood.

You do not need graphic language or description to write a hot sex scene. What you do need is evocative language and a strong grasp of your characters and what emotions the scene is supposed to convey.

Every word you use in a sex scene must add to the mood, remember?

Don't pass up the chance to use it as effectively as possible, and don't feel you have to go beyond your comfort zone to turn people on. That *Cruel as the Grave* scene made my heart pound, I can promise you. You can have the same effect on your readers simply by writing about passion and emotion; you don't need to write about physical actions if you don't want.

But you have to give them something.

So, here's an assignment. Remember the scenes you wrote before with just pure physical emotion? Pull that out again (heh heh, see, I plan ahead!) Does it really need the physical stuff?

Find a book with a not-so-graphic scene that turns you on or you particularly like. What about it gets you? Is that something you feel you can bring in to your work?

Write a very graphic scene, with dialogue, graphic language, whatever you like. Now try rewriting it using the cleanest—but still evocative—language you can. Does the scene still work?

Part 13: More on chemistry and character

Now. Several people pointed out to me last time that the Sharon Kay Penman scene didn't do it for them. Several more mentioned that if they knew the characters better, it probably would have.

Which is exactly the point that I've made here, a few times (and I'm not being bitchy; I was really pleased to see those comments because A. It proved me right, and I do so love to be right; B. It shows y'all are really paying attention; and C. It shows you guys are really absorbing and feel comfortable speaking up—you're really getting your own ideas on what works and what doesn't, and what you would do differently, and why something does or does not work for you. Which is AWESOME).

Remember the "bold statement" in the "Chemistry" post? There were two of them, actually; the first was

A sex scene is the culmination of everything the hero/heroine have done, said, and been through together from the moment they meet (or the moment the reader meets them)."

The second was

Your Hero/heroine should react to and interact with each other. If they don't do that, nobody's going to be interested in seeing them have sex."

This is where erotic romance has a bit of an advantage, simply because it is so graphic, and the more graphic a scene is, the easier it is to turn someone on with it.

But every sex scene is hotter if the reader is involved, and I chose those two examples to illustrate that point. You can—and should—involve them with evocative language, with rhythm, with imagery (we're doing that soon), with a little dialogue, with emotion, sensation, and thought; there are lots of ways to do it and lots of little tricks you should be using. But the number one most important point is to emotionally involve the reader *before* the sex occurs.

Now, I appreciate this is my blog, and my work, and I'm obviously not posting it for critique—what would be the point? *Blood Will Tell* was published over a year ago; *Eighth Wand* ten months ago (at the time of this writing). It's not like I'm going to go back and edit them at this point, not when they've each already sold several thousand copies in ebook format. BUT. I expect that each and every one of you noticed something missing in the scenes I've quoted (perhaps not as much with the *Eighth Wand* scene, as it was a dialogue-heavy scene and I gave you some background first.)

But certainly Monday's *BWT* scene—especially as it too was a very emotional scene, actually—suffered for lack of your personal emotional involvement with the characters.

Remember what we said the other day, about the difference between pornography and erotica/erotic romance? The difference is emotion.

A sex scene without emotion, no matter how well written, is just a cheap thrill. You must involve the reader first. You must make them anticipate.

Now, again, we're starting to really reach a point where the topics are so intertwined it's hard to separate them. I don't want to go too much into foreplay, because we're doing foreplay in depth week after next. We've already discussed chemistry and emotion, but we still need to view everything through those lenses. And it's hard to talk about imagery and allusion here when we'll be doing them next week, along with actual mechanics—

what goes where when, how to avoid making it sound like somebody has three hands, that sort of thing.

So honestly? I think I'm going to cut this one short. I feel kind of guilty about that, because I try to give you 1500 words and this is just over half that. But it's two am here (I was baking and decorating a birthday cake, plus I'm an insomniac), and I have to be up at like eight in the morning for the birthday stuff. So I hope you guys can forgive me.

Note: Part 14 was a guest post on submissive men by Emily Veinglory. I don't own the rights to it, but it is still on the blog, at http://www.staciakane.net/2008/08/11/be-a-sex-writing-strumpet-pt-14-guest-blog/ if you'd like to read it--and it is worth reading!

Part 15, Imagery and Allusion: making your scene mean something

Obviously, your scene is going to mean something no matter what—at least, it should. But by adding imagery and allusion, by bringing something bigger and more universal to the scene, you can heighten the tension and hopefully give the readers something special, something to imprint the scene in their minds.

With *Personal Demons*, for example, I used fire. Now I'm not saying fire imagery is the most original idea in the world—it is emphatically not, and I normally use it very sparingly to avoid cliché. But because Greyson Dante was a fire demon, it worked for the scene (at least I think it did.) More importantly, though, the fire imagery allowed me to give readers an extremely important clue about Megan and her connection to the demon world. Remember this line?

She opened her mouth and hot smoke escaped with her cries of ecstasy.

Huge clue, right? How did that manage to happen if Megan was entirely human? And it was because the scene established that (thus giving the story another push forward, btw; if the sex scene did nothing else in the book it was necessary because it was the only way I could implant that clue without it being hugely obvious, and I wanted it to be subtle) that I was able to make so much use of the fire imagery.

Megan felt it literally, because it was Greyson's energy, pushing into her and imprinting on her soul. There were literal flames in the room, around the ceiling. There were virtual ones before Megan's eyes and in her body, and the entire scene was designed not just to please the reader but to plant a little seed there. If you read the scene again you'll see how the energy works (and what the erotic potential of it is). In all, I'm very proud of that scene because I packed it with as much information as I think I possibly could, and I think it's a hot little scene to boot.

It doesn't have to be fire, and your hero/ine doesn't have to have spiffy sex powers (well, okay, *somebody* should have some spiffy sex powers—at least until we get to comical/non-arousing sex scenes—but they don't have to be the magical kind).

In fact, as I said above, it probably shouldn't be fire and it really shouldn't be water (again, unless water is a big part of your story); trust me, comparing an orgasm to the ocean wave crashing over your character isn't going to win you any prizes for originality. That doesn't mean you can't make it work, just that it will be harder. (Oh, but—*everything should be wet*. Wet is sexy. Just be careful with the Jacques Cousteau stuff.)

What does your story focus on, and how can you bring that focus into your scene? Remember, the scene must be a cohesive part of the book. It must stay in voice, it must stay in character. It should be seamless. So what imagery do you use throughout the rest of the story, and how can you use it for sex?

Let's take, for example...okay. Let's see what I can make up here. Let's take a straight contemporary (which I don't like writing, so give me a break here, this is an example not a candidate for an award) in which the heroine often thinks of or sees the hero as a pirate. He's not a pirate, and obviously you don't want to step too hard on that imagery throughout the book, but you as the writer (or I as the writer) have subtly used piratey images and comparisons throughout in the heroine's POV.

Like, she sees him as "swarthy," or "he walks like he should have a cutlass strapped to his waist" or maybe "he grinned like a pirate who'd just found some free gold." Maybe he can say something like, "When I see something I want I take it," and the heroine can then call him a pirate. That sort of thing; you want to be careful with it, because you don't want readers to roll their eyes and go, "Yeah, we freaking *get it*, okay? Pirate. Yadda yadda yadda," but you can plant a seed in the reader's mind here and there, right?

I've been building wolf imagery around a character for some time; no one has ever commented on it but I bet if I mentioned it they'd see it immediately (of course, it could just be that either I'm too subtle with it, or everyone noticed it, hated it, and didn't say anything because they were so embarrassed by its heavy-handedness).

Anyway, let's get back to our piratey investment banker or whatever he is, and his Wall Street broker ladyfriend. What might he do, that we can bring a touch of pirate to the scene? (If you suggest having him shout, "ARRR!" when he comes I will slap you.)

Okay, there's some obvious ones. He can make her feel special, caress her like she's a precious jewel or a treasure. He could call her that, if he's that type of guy. You can bring words into the scene like glittering, or gold, or treasure, or (*don'tsaybootydon'tsaybootydon'tsaybooty*) hook—yes, you can use that, he could hook her with his hand or she could hook her leg around him. You can bring to her mind images of empty nights at sea, the rocking of boats, the breeze off the Caribbean. You can have him take her, steal her, rob her of her inhibitions or shame; he could even plunder her (mm, I think plunder is a sexy word). Hell, you can have him smell like rum if you want to, as long as there's a good reason for it (lots of men wear bay rum cologne/aftershave, in fact; it used to be a staple, and I actually love it).

There's any number of ways you can bring these images into the scene, and any number of ways you can use them. But you want to do something, because your scene cannot exist in a vacuum. By pulling threads you've laid before, by reminding the reader of certain words and images, you not only make the scene much more cohesive and interesting, you make it unique. It's about these characters, these two people, with their specific tastes and smells and memories and thoughts, not about anyone else.

Here are a few images, though, that do not generally belong in sex scenes. This may be personal taste, but I have seen them attempted in the past and found them at best unsexy, at worst distasteful:

*Anything at all to do with fish

*Anything at all to do with children (unless you're in your final love scenes and the characters are thinking how lovely it would be to make a baby. NO imagery of childhood belongs within ten feet of sex; call me a prude or whatever, but it simply doesn't work for me).

*Little furry animals (Yes, I know all about furries, and as Miss Brodie would say, for people who like that sort of thing, that is the sort of thing they like. But I don't want to be thinking about bunnies and puppies when I'm supposed to be getting turned on).

*Any implication that various orifices are used for purposes other than sexual (again, in a funny or unsexy scene, this may be useful, but not in a sexy one. And see Miss Brodie's quote above if you disagree. You don't need me to tell you this anyway, right? If poop turns you on I think you're already aware you're in the minority).

*No thinking of family members, please What else can you think of?

Make the scene unique by bringing your characters' unique viewpoints into play. Remember, no matter what the logistics of actual physical intercourse are, no two couples have sex exactly the same way.

Every word and image you use in your story should contribute to characterization, relationship, and plot. So it is with your sex scene. Use the bricks you've already laid; it will make the scene that much more appealing, interesting, and arousing to your readers. It will make the scene belong to your characters alone.

Part 16, Whose hand is that?

So. I'm actually having a bit of a hard time with this one, because it's basic. You're writing an action scene, so you need to make sure the physical action flows and makes sense. If a hand appears, the reader needs to know whose hand it is. This is especially important when writing ménage-and-more type scenes (and btw, it occurred to me that in Monday's post I mentioned that the scene is about two people, and have repeatedly throughout referred to H/h or two people. This is simply for ease in writing and brevity; it's not meant to imply in any way, shape or form that scenes should or have to only involve two people. I've written a few ménage books, as you guys know, and like them just fine and in my case they were certainly romances. Just wanted to get that on the record).

So. A sex scene is an action scene, and you need to make sure the action flows and fits the scene. How do you do that? What exactly are they doing, anyway? (We're going to work on choreography etc. later, too, this is just an intro).

Here's where the potential problem comes in. Because we've pretty much all had sex, and because we're intimately familiar with the act (no pun intended) and with what we're writing, it's easy to slip and create body parts out of thin air. Or forget to mention something. Bad sex writing often isn't just clunky or drab; it's laughable, because it can create such odd images in the reader's head, even more so, I think, than other bad writing.

I can't for the life of me remember where I saw this, but I will never forget reading on a blog or something an example of bad sex writing. It was something about the hero "spreading the twin lobes of [the heroine's] clitoris." Ummm... Yeah.

But most mistakes aren't that bad, or that obvious. They're things that make perfect sense to you, the writer, because you see it in your head. For example, you might think it's very hot to have the hero lift the heroine and brace her against the wall—and it totally can be—but if his hands are under her thighs, it is impossible for him to then grab her breast unless you mention he shifts his grip. Yes, it's the type of thing you'd expect the reader to know—too-detailed sex writing is bad too—but you really should at least give the reader some clue. So here's some common mistakes:

*If the hero is physically inside the heroine, he cannot lick, suck, or kiss her bellybutton. Breasts I'll buy, depending on the height difference and how limber he is (although I've seen editors and readers ding writers for that too, so be careful) but there is absolutely no way his cock is inside her and his mouth is anywhere near her stomach. Try it out with your partner, seriously.

*If you're writing a ménage, you need to use names. It might be very clear to you which "he" is behind the heroine and which "he" is in front, but once somebody grabs her hair we need to know who it is—unless you're going for a "She wasn't sure which one and didn't care because of the blissBlissBLISS" sort of thing. Using names all the time can sound clunky, but trust me, you'd much rather use names than have your readers laugh or get confused.

*If the heroine is giving the hero head, he cannot do the same to her unless you specify she is turned around or have him turn her around.

*Nobody's arms reach their feet when they're lying down flat.

*If the hero is much taller than the heroine, they can certainly kiss while having sex but not with their chests pressed together. (Trust me on that. My husband is a foot taller than me.)

    *Also with the height difference thing, if he's much taller and they're standing up, he needs to seriously bend his knees or she needs to find something to brace her feet on or something.

    *Two men cannot enter the heroine from behind at once.

    *Clothes have to come off or be otherwise out of the way. You don't have to describe this in detail, at all; I've blogged before about how my heroes rarely wear underwear simply because I hate writing removal of male underwear. You can say "Her clothes seemed to melt away under his skillful hands;" you can have the hero tear her panties off; whatever you like. It's supposed to be sexy, not a laundry list. But the reader is not going to just assume they're naked if you don't at least give a hint.

    *Beware of phantom body parts; keep a clear picture in your head of what everyone is doing and where their hands and feet etc. are.

    What others can you think of?

    I know quite a few writers who use books like the Kama Sutra or The Joy of Sex to help them choreograph and write sex scenes. I never actually have, but somewhere I've got a sex book (that my MOTHER gave me, no shit) with lots of nice pictures of different positions and stuff. Books like that—guides—are worth checking out. Porn really isn't, at least not for these purposes. Because porn is a fantasy. The job of a pornographic actor or actress is to make the sex look hot; it doesn't matter if they're cold or uncomfortable or their back hurts or their arms feel like they're going to pop out of their sockets, they have to look like they're having a great time. It may be a great visual to have a woman balance on one leg on a railing while somebody nails her from behind, but a reader is going to think of the physical awkwardness of it simply because s/he can't see the character's face.

There is a lot more to cover on this topic but it intersperses with stuff we'll be doing through the remainder of the series, so apologies that this installment isn't everything it could be. We *will* get there. For now I just wanted to get some basic stuff out of the way.

Beware of phantom body parts or bodies doing things they physically cannot; re-read the scene slowly. Act it out (literally, heh heh, or even with dolls or your hands or whatever. Make sure you're giving the reader something real to picture.

I do want to touch very quickly on POV here as well. We'll do more on that close to the end—I don't think POV is a very involved topic, frankly—but someone asked about writing from the male POV so here's my thoughts on it. I love writing from the male POV, especially sex. And I find it fairly easy to do; of course, they're my sex scenes and I like them, so of course this is something I think I'm good at, but the reviewers seem to agree. And there is a bit of a trick to writing sex from a male's POV, sure, but it's an easy one.

All you have to do is ask yourself what you want a man to be thinking when he's having sex with you.

Do you want him to be worshipful, reverent? Do you want him to be thinking this moment feels like forever? Do you want him to be thinking how beautiful you are? How good you smell?

What type of man are you writing? A big Alpha who's always in control? What would the reaction of a man like that be, to discover during sex that he's losing that control?

Now, you don't want to go too overboard with this. Remember, he's still a man. He's not going to be picturing unicorns and rainbows. But he is going to be seeing the heroine a certain way, without flaws. He is going to be overwhelmed by certain things about her. He is going to feel things, just the way the heroine does. She feels him stretch her inner walls and fill her up; he feels those walls grip him and surround him with wet heat. She feels his chest hot and hard against hers; he feels her breasts crush against his skin.

What I've just done there, with the little examples, is something I like to do a lot. I mirror their thoughts and sensations. If he sees her, even for a dizzy moment, as some sort of goddess he's worshipping with his body, I like her to think of herself that way or that he makes her feel that way. It's a way of demonstrating to the reader how in-tune they are. It adds depth and cohesiveness to the scene, and again, makes the scene uniquely theirs.

Writing sex is just like writing any other action scene; you must make sure the actions flow and are physically possible. You don't have to get fancy, but you do have to make sure everyone's body parts are accounted for and everything makes sense.

You don't want people laughing at your sex scene.

Part 17: What Part of Sex is Sexy?

Okay, so we've looked into why your sex scene is there, language, rhythm, and the expansion of character and relationship, so it's time to start the really fun stuff and talk about amping up the sexiness of your sex scenes. We'll do more of this as we go along, but I wanted to slide us into it easily today, to make us all ready and willing. To prepare us, if you will. To make us desperate for more. In other words, to talk about foreplay.

The thing is, while writing about sex usually involves penetration, covering the physical act of penetration is the least important part of writing the scene. And it's the least interesting. And I honestly believe this is where a lot of people slip up. Because, despite my strong belief that no two people make love the exact same way as far as their feelings and emotions etc. etc. go, the fact is, once Tab A is inserted into Slot B, all that's left—physically—is a little friction.

Obviously when writing that friction—as we've already covered—you add emotion and sensation, thought, allusion, and imagery to make that friction interesting and different (as do different positions etc.-- having sex from behind, for example, is a very different experience from face-to-face; it looks different, it feels different physically and emotionally).

But the longest sex scene possible—I believe *Blood Will Tell*'s bathroom scene is one of the longest instances of penetration I've written—is still going to be much shorter than foreplay. Like in real life, foreplay can go on for pages and pages; penetration is probably not going to last longer than a page or two--twenty or thirty minutes tops (and let's be somewhat realistic here; do you really want it to? Chafing isn't fun. Neither is numbness. I've never understood people who go on and on about hours of tantric sex; I have stuff to *do*. I'm fully aware that may just be me, but really, whether it's in real life or in books, there's only so much you can do once the actual business gets started).

I've never consciously planned this, but in thinking back I think my scenes on average are about 70-80% foreplay. Of course every scene is different. I'm a fan of rough, fast, must-have-you-now scenes, but I would say the majority of my scenes hover in that percentage.

Foreplay doesn't have to be achingly long hours of teasing and kissing and touching, either. Here's a bit of foreplay from *Black Dragon*, my attempt at an "old school" medieval romance (not only does this have a different voice from my usual work, because it's an old-school historical, but it's from Cerridwen Press so is one of my less graphic scenes; it also contains a minor linguistic anachronism or two [which I explained in the book's Author's Note, lest you think me lazy]):

"I hate you," she said, tears in her eyes at both the cruelty and truth of his words. "I wish we had never met, I wish we had never married, I wish I had never come here."

"Aye? Then that makes two of us, my lady, for I do not like you much either."

"You do not like anyone, including yourself," she snapped. "Tell me, Gruffydd, what happened to you in life that made you so eager to grow up to be a complete bastard? You are certainly ready enough to examine my flaws. How about yours? How about the way you refuse to show any vulnerability, as if you can be more than human simply by willing it so? The way you will not allow anything to be important to you?"

"Stop."

"I will not. How about the way you hate having people help you in any way? How about the secrets you keep? Finding out what you want for your meal is a trial, much less anything about you or your life. You say I like to hide behind a façade and then tell myself nobody understands me. I am not surprised you see this, my lord, for I have never in my life met someone who hides as much as you do!"

"Stop it."

"What else are you hiding, Gruffydd? What other ways do you devise to cause pain to yourself, to—"

"Stop it!" he yelled. His fists were clenched at his sides.

"Oh, are you angry? Are you actually showing some feeling? Forgive me, you have never done so before and I fear I am not seeing correctly."

"Stop it, Isabelle, or I swear I will—"

"You'll what? Hit me? I would not be surprised if you did. I have been expecting it since the day we met."

"Do not tempt me!"

He grabbed her shoulders, his gaze burning into hers, rooting her to where she now stood. Livid at both him and the fire started in her belly by his mere touch, she twisted sideways, struggling to pull free from the feelings in her heart and body. But he pulled her closer, making escape from the heat of his skin and the strength of his hands impossible. She gasped.

For a moment they stared at each other, their faces furious, chests heaving in unison, before his mouth fell on hers, devouring her lips as his grip threatened to squeeze the life from her body.

Now, I know the fight-into-sex isn't exactly original (nor is the "Don't tempt me!" line--it's pretty cliche but so what?), but I don't care. I love it. I love writing angry sex, because angry people are people with less inhibitions, people whose passions are already raised.

That's why I'm using this particular scene; it shows you don't have to write traditional foreplay for the reader to still believe these people are ready for some sex. I'm particularly proud of this scene because it enables me to do a couple of very important things, and show how well the characters know each other (Gruffydd's analysis of Isabelle's character came immediately before this and sparked her tirade, but would be too long to excerpt here); it also gives the reader an additional insight to Gruffydd's character because, although Isabelle doesn't know it, he self-harms, which makes her comment about him devising other ways to cause pain to himself extra sharp and explains why he goes from angry to furious in about a second and a half. (And, true to form, the actual sex part of that scene is only a few paragraphs of raging, angry, violent sex; 70-80%, remember? Not a rule, but a guideline.)

So in this bit of foreplay we see the characters know each other well. They've obviously spent time watching each other and paying attention to each other, even if they won't admit it. Spending that amount of time studying someone indicates passionate feelings; we don't absorb that much about people to whom we're indifferent. It also shows us the relationship at something of an impasse: because they've had sex once before, they now find it difficult-to-impossible to be around each other under any degree of emotion or stress without touching, but neither of them is willing to acknowledge it. They're using sex to solve their problem, in other words, and the problem is they can't admit their feelings.

I know the effect here is a bit deadened because you haven't read the book and so aren't familiar with the characters, but in the book itself, again if I've done my job, by the time Gruffydd plants that kiss on Isabelle the reader's heart is pounding too, from the emotional intensity of the moment. And like any other stress or high emotion, it's easy to translate that into sexual intensity.

Just like the rest of the sex scene, foreplay must advance the relationship; it must advance the story; it must interest and arouse. How you do that is up to you; the above example is just one way (we're going to get into more traditional foreplay Wednesday and some writing tips and examples on Friday.)

Honestly, since the sex scene is the culmination of every moment the characters have shared up until then, you could say the entire book is foreplay—and as we discussed in the last post, you can and should bring images and thoughts from their previous interactions into the sex scene, in order to make the entire thing more cohesive.

Foreplay is where your characters assert their individuality. It's what makes this scene uniquely theirs, and not anyone else's. And just like real life, it's terribly important.

So. Find a published sex scene you particularly like, but this time focus on the foreplay. What is it about the foreplay in that scene that does it for you? Is it very sexy, and why? Is it clever, or funny, or angry? Find several scenes; is the foreplay similar in those scenes, or very different? What is the foreplay-to-penetration ratio of your favorite scenes?

Take one of the scenes you've written and re-read it, stopping as soon as penetration occurs. How much foreplay is there? Have you stretched it out long enough, is it as intense as it should/could be, or does the real action start when the real action starts? Is that ratio the same for all of your sex scenes, and if so, how can you mix it up a bit? Remember, not every scene has to be 70-80% foreplay, not at all. But if you're looking to heat up your scenes, expanding the foreplay should be the first thing you look at.

Part 18, Foreplay 2: Who are you?

As we discussed Monday, a large portion of your sex scene is probably going to be foreplay. You've spent your entire book, or at least large chunks of it, preparing the reader for this; so how do you bring it all home? By being true to your characters, and writing the scene as honestly as you can.

Now, of course some things in a sex scene are a bit idealized. Nobody ever has bad breath. Everybody comes, often more than once (for the women, anyway). Everybody smells good (more on that in a minute), men almost never need more than a few moment's encouragement to get hard...it's a lovely world, really, and not always true-to-life, but you must be honest when it comes to your characters' emotions. Because those emotions drive the scene and make it theirs; those emotions develop and strengthen their characters and their relationship.

Monday we looked at an atypical foreplay scene, a big fight. So today we'll focus on more "traditional" foreplay. Here's a snippet from *Blood Will Tell*. I think it's still a bit unusual in that it doesn't include any oral sex, but let's see what you guys think:

He put his arm back around her and pulled her close, so her head rested on his chest. Under the covers, his legs snaked around hers. The hair on his thighs rubbed against her own smooth legs, sending shivers of delight through her entire body.

"Julian?"

"Yes?"

She flipped over so that she straddled him, her hands braced on the smooth muscles of his bare chest. His cock stirred beneath her and she gave a little wiggle, making him gasp.

Cecelia smiled, suddenly determined to show Mr. Mansfield what kind of woman he was dealing with. "I think it's my turn to be on top."

She centered herself over the hard shaft of Julian's now-erect cock and moved forward slightly. He sighed softly as her wet lips stroked over the head and back down again, and she sighed as well when her clit came in contact with the silken skin covering the head of his dick.

His hands slid between her legs to toy with her clit, then rose up to play with her nipples, tugging them gently with fingers covered in her own juices. She dropped her head back and let her hands fall, lightly running over the head of his cock before they reached the trimmed hair of her mound. She separated her lips and began gently pulling at them, glancing down to see Julian watching her hands, his face transformed by lust.

"You are amazing," he whispered, as she slid her index finger down over her clit and began rubbing it lightly. The sensation of being watched combined with what she was doing made her incredibly hot, and she let her eyes fall closed as she continued teasing herself with her fingers. Her hips started moving, her wet pussy sliding deliciously along the length of his cock, fiery and rigid against her own soft flesh.

"Cecelia." He grabbed her hips, pulling her upward so that he could fit himself inside her.

She pulled away. "Not yet," she whispered, enjoying the frustration on his face. "I'm in charge here."

"Oh, Jesus," he groaned, throwing his head back on the pillow and closing his eyes.

She grinned. "Patience is a virtue."

"It's not one I want to learn." He gasped as she ground herself harder on his rampant cock, teasing him by letting the tip slide just into her entrance then pulling away again. His fingers dug more deeply into her hips, but he did not try to move her again. He was letting her control things, at least for the moment, and Cecelia enjoyed the power in a way she never had before. Watching Julian's reaction to her was incredibly sexy. She rubbed against him faster, his gasps filling her ears, her blood racing as her clit became more and more sensitive and engorged against his cock.

She leaned back, her full breasts moving gently, her erect nipples dark red against her pale skin. She reached down behind her and let her fingernails scratch gently up his inner thighs. His hips jerked up beneath her, and when she ran her nails across his balls he groaned.

"Enough," he growled, and before she knew what was happening he lifted her up again and impaled her in one smooth, quick thrust.

(I used "dick" in that scene; in retrospect I wish I hadn't, btw, but I used cock so much I needed some variety.)

So what do we notice here? First, there's a lot of dialogue. I think it's fairly sexy dialogue, too. I also think that for those of you who haven't read *BWT*, it gives you a fairly good picture of what the Julian/Cecelia relationship is, or at least has been before this: lots of banter, with Julian dominant (I still think he got two of the best lines I've ever written for a hero, btw; right before their very first kiss Cecelia says, "Wait a minute. I don't even think I like you," and he replies, "You don't have to." Later she tells him her mother warned her about men like him and he says, "Let's go back to my place. I'll show you why she was right." Sigh).

Second, this is Cecelia's conscious attempt to assert some authority, to stop being Julian's sex toy and start being a strong woman. How do you think it worked? What do you think it says about her that she feels confident enough to do that, what does it say about the relationship and her hopes for it that she feels the need to do that?

For me, what makes this scene still a bit atypical is that it doesn't include any oral sex. Oral sex is one of the touchstones of foreplay, IMO; if you recall, this entire series started because I was thinking about oral sex and whether everyone has to trade off equally all the time. I don't think they do, personally. I'm happy to assume they're both getting and giving some, I don't need to see it every time. And yes, to me, as a woman, it's far more important that I see the woman get hers than it is to see the man get his. I'm pleased by both, but as I said in that long-ago blow job post, the woman is the partner who isn't guaranteed an orgasm from penetration; she's the one who can come and still have sex immediately after. Logistically it makes more sense, and emotionally it makes more sense; if he isn't even going to make sure she comes he's kind of a jerk.

For this reason I am intensely annoyed when I read heroines in romance or other genres—I haven't seen this in a while but it seemed to be all the rage at one point—who really enjoy, um, manual stimulation but don't like having oral sex performed on them for whatever reason.

Who are these women? More to the point, who are the men who've been giving them head in the past? Because seriously, if you can't arouse a woman that way, you are really doing something wrong. (Yes, this is a total digression.) It's oral sex, it's not rocket science (incidentally, I was so pleased with that line that I almost used it for the title of this post. Oral Sex: It's not Rocket Science); the heroine-who-doesn't-enjoy-it always feels to me like a projection of the writer's discomfort with sex or her own ladyparts, or a cheap "modern" way of using that old romance trope of "I never really liked sex until HE came along, sigh." I don't particularly like writing those heroines and I don't particularly like reading them.

I can buy a virginal heroine being nervous or uncomfortable with oral sex, sure, but not a woman who's supposed to be at least somewhat experienced (and again, if you want to make her nervousness or discomfort part of her character that's fine; just don't suddenly yank this "I hate oral sex" crap out of your hat because you, the writer, aren't comfortable writing an oral scene or think it makes your hero look Especially Manly or whatever. Making her uncomfortable is fine, if there's a reason for it, especially if you've set that reason up and made it a part of her character. It can be incredibly hot to have the hero explain exactly what he's going to do to her and how very much he wants to do it; if he's that type of guy, go for it.

The simple fact is, women should like oral sex and a true hero wants to give it. End of story. A man who doesn't want to do it, or who makes derogatory statements about it, is not a hero; he is a jerk. (I will never forget reading a snippet of a book where the hero looks up from his task and admonishes the heroine for not keeping her pubic hair properly trimmed. If a man did that to me I would have done a damn good impersonation of Van Damme cracking a guy's skull between his thighs.)

A heroine who won't give head is not a heroine I want to know; she's prissy and frigid. Sorry, I realize I've digressed all over the place, but that's why foreplay gets its own week instead of just one post.

The point is, foreplay is a golden opportunity to really get into your characters' heads. Don't wimp out on it. Even if they're just saying some nice things to each other, even if they're barely speaking, every word and every action counts.

This is your chance to have the hero or heroine really take charge; it's your chance to show how well they know each other; it's your chance to show them interacting as people, just people. Be honest about who they are and what they want; show their weaknesses as well as their strengths.

Maybe someone is shy about their body. Maybe someone is so desperate they can barely speak. Maybe there's anger there, or sadness. Remember how we can illuminate subtext through sex? That's especially true of foreplay.

Your readers are not going to enjoy and be aroused by your foreplay if the characters themselves are not. Use this opportunity; let them do what they want. Your readers will thank you for it.

Try writing some sexy dialogue for your characters. Really think about what they might say, and how to make it theirs.

Write a scene where the hero is simply stroking the heroine's body. First from his POV, then hers. No dialogue. What are they thinking? How does what they think play itself out through their actions?

Part 19, Foreplay 3: Tips, tricks, and hints

Just as everyone likes different things in bed, everyone is going to like different things in written sex and foreplay. I've never made any bones about the fact that certain things just turn me off; I try very hard to keep my sex scenes what I consider classy. Erotic and hot, rather than crude—even when my characters are being crude there are places I don't go. For example, although there's nothing inherently wrong with having the hero manually stimulate the heroine and then lick his fingers, it squicks me out a little so I don't write it (in fact, there is never any evidence on the hero's face that he has just performed oral sex, because yuck. At least to me. This is what women's thighs and bellies are for; he can kiss and nuzzle them until he's nice and clean. Again, some women find the evidence sexy, and I certainly don't mean and am not implying that they're crude or disgusting because of it; come on, I find the idea of the hero drinking the heroine's blood hot, so I'm hardly one to judge. It's just something I don't find arousing so I don't write it. I don't use phrases like "eat pussy" and I don't have characters say things like that either. Again, personal taste. No pun intended.)

But just as we drop linguistic hints throughout the book of how hot or "open" the sex scene is going to be, we really do this with foreplay. Once the kissin' starts, the reader learns exactly what s/he is in for, so make it count.

And what about kissing? We've talked so much about talking and cunnilingus and cocks, we've barely talked about kissing at all. It's funny; although kissing is a huge part of a sex scene I never really think of it that way, I guess because my characters have usually kissed at least a couple of times before the sexing starts. But what about those kisses? Are they soft, delicate brushes of the lips, gradually gaining in intensity as each person feels how much the other wants this? Or are they crushing, passionate, bruising? (I know there are people who think things like "bruising kisses" are lame and cliché. But you know what? Things don't become cliché if people don't like reading them. I love the bruising, breathless kiss and will never give it up, personally.)

What about touching? Not just touching intimate parts, either (although of course, there's lots of fun to be had from delving into those wet folds or gently grasping that hot, hard, thick cock already slick with desire). Does the hero bury his hands in the heroine's hair? Does he stroke her face, her throat? Her ribcage? Does he skim his hands over her breasts, and how does she react—does she grab his wrist to hold it there (which can show she's comfortable with him and her sexuality and wants more) or does she pull away? Does she have a moment to think how she wishes her breasts were bigger or smaller or prettier, is she that type of girl? Or is she absolutely confident that he finds every bit of her beautiful?

Where are her hands? Does she run them over his board shoulders, or press them against his chest, feeling how different his body is, how hard and manly he is? (Hey, I actually do think stuff like that, and I bet I'm not the only woman in the world who does. We like how different your bodies are, men, and we want to emphasize that, just as I'm sure you like how different our bodies are). Does she feel the heavy muscles of his back under his skin? Slide her hands down to his firm ass (or bottom, or whatever—I rarely use "ass" in a sex scene, I'm not sure why), or over his narrow hips to the front? If he's hairy does she play with the hair, feel it under her fingers, tickling her sensitive skin like a thousand little electric shocks?

Who undresses whom, and how? In *Personal Demons*, Greyson—being the little hedonist that he is—takes time to undress Megan slowly; he wants to enjoy every second of it, to savor what's about to happen, but when it comes to his own clothing he just wants it off and tears the buttons of his shirt to get it that way. He also has her remove the garter belt and stockings she was wearing; why do you think he does that? A lot of men would have wanted her to leave it on (and there's absolutely nothing wrong with that, because obviously garter belts and stockings are very sexy and what man wouldn't want to see his woman in them? I love wearing them myself).

What does it say about him that at least this time he wants her completely naked, so he can see and touch every inch of her? (I'd actually be very interested in anyone's thoughts on that; it surprised me a little when I wrote it.)

But what about your characters? Do they tear at each other's clothing? Do they leave a trail of discarded garments across the floor, or a heap by the bed? Are there articles of clothing they don't even bother to remove at all (shirts, socks, panties still around an ankle, what)? I think half-dressed sex can be incredibly hot, especially if the clothing constricts movement.

Where do they kiss each other? Earlobes, necks, collarbones? Stomachs? The hipbone is incredibly sensitive on men and women; nibbling it always evokes a response in both the character and the reader who's had it done to them and remembers what it feels like. What about toes and feet and legs? Hands? I've never been a fan of writing finger-sucking simply because once the finger is in the mouth it can be awkward to pull it out. But you can do it, and simply replace the thumb with her mouth or whatever, thus skimming over the awkward stuff. Does he suck her breasts and nipples? Hard or soft? Slow or fast? Does she bite his chest gently? Does she suck on or otherwise play with his nipples? A lot of men like that, too.

And what about oral sex? What is he doing with that mouth of his? Savoring, sucking, nibbling? Exploring, teasing, tasting? Slipping his tongue inside in a shallow rhythm? Does he pull her plump, hard little clit into his mouth? What does she do when she comes, when she feels herself getting ready to? Is she a bold woman who buries her fingers in his hair and presses him closer, or is she biting her fingers or palm or gripping the pillow or fisting the sheets in her sweaty, trembling hands? Is he holding her legs open, or caressing her breasts? Are her feet propped on his shoulders?

How about when she goes down on him? Is he gathering her hair in tender hands, holding it above her head, out of the way? Is he watching, and if so, what does he see and how does she feel about it? Does it turn her on to know he's watching? Does she look up and meet his eyes? How intense is that? Is she running her fingernails over his balls, scratching lightly? How about his inner thighs? Is she just sucking his cock or is she letting her tongue play over the top, down the heavy, hard length of him? Does she vary her speed or the depth? Does she flutter her tongue over that little skin ridge on the underside, or down to his sac? Does she pull one of his balls into her mouth? If you're writing a very graphic scene, is she bringing her fingers into play at his rear entrance? How does he feel about all this—safe, sexy, incredibly turned on, desperate?

When you write foreplay or sex, you're inviting the reader to experience what the characters experience (hell, when you write any book you do that, but you know what I mean). You want to use things the reader has felt, seen, tasted, smelled, as well as evocative words and dialogue and all that other stuff, to evoke a physical and

emotional response. In short, you want to turn them on. So think of writing foreplay as trying to get your partner into bed. What do you do? What are the buttons you have to press?

Describe everything! Foreplay and sex is where you can let your language go; be as evocative and descriptive as you can (next week we'll do another list of words to help get you going).

Foreplay is your chance to write a long, hot scene where nobody gets too graphic if you don't want to. For example, most of the lines and suggestions I've made above are more graphic; they're ideas for you to use as well as wording suggestions. But you can write an oral scene where he kisses down her stomach—spend some time on it, make her really feel and think about it—and then "his mouth moved against her, his tongue, so hot, so wet (remember, *everything should be wet!*)...she'd never felt anything like it before. He teased her, tormented her, calling from her sounds she didn't know she could make and feelings she didn't realize she could feel, until her entire body convulsed and she was left breathless, her heart pounding, floating somewhere above the bed in a delicious daze." See? Nary a four-letter word in there, but we all know what happened and that it was good.

So. Take a good hard look at your foreplay scenes. Where can you expand them? How much do your characters move? You don't want anyone to ever be still; that's not sexy. Keep them moving! Are they feeling every bit of what's happening, thinking about it, tasting it, experiencing? Are they truly interacting or does it feel like they're bloodless paper dolls? Remember, oral sex is more than a few quick dips of the head—it should generally be more in your scenes as well. Take your time, and let your characters take their time if they're so inclined. I promise you, most of what turns your readers on will be foreplay; just like in real life, don't think you need to hurry up and get to The Good Stuff. This *is* the good stuff!

Find a published foreplay scene you particularly like. What are those characters doing? How is what they do different from a scene you don't like; is it language or graphicness or is it something deeper, something you're just not connecting with? Why do you think you didn't connect with it? Take those pure-touching scenes you wrote Wednesday and add some interaction. If he's thinking how beautiful she is while he strokes her breast, how lucky he is or how much he wants her, how do his thoughts intensify when he sees her ladyparts? What does he want to do with those? Likewise, if she's touching his muscled chest or the thin line of hair on his abdomen, how does she feel when she sees his cock there? What is she anticipating? Write it down! Write it all in there!

Part 20: What exactly are they doing?

Anyway. So we're basically done with foreplay, but today's topic is still part of it, and leads into the rest of the series. BTW, I've got four topics left to cover.

One of the things I tried to subtly impress upon you in the last post was the importance of descriptive words. Go read it again if you're not sure what I mean (Go ahead. I'll wait). I know we've discussed language a few times, in a few different variations, already, so we've already touched on this and alluded to it. But I really, strongly feel that the two keys to a hot sex scene are smoking chemistry and evocative language, so you'll have to put up with me talking about it again.

Because this post isn't just about evocative words or action words. It's about description.

In "normal" writing we try to keep description at a certain level. We need it, of course. A book with no descriptions isn't a book, it's a script (and even those have a level of description). But we can't go overboard. Every step someone takes can't be purposeful, every touch can't be gentle, every movement can't be fluid.

But a sex scene is about emotion and sensation. It's about building a certain rhythm with your words. Sometimes you need to add words to make that rhythm work; sometimes you need to take them away. But they have to flow, and they have to draw the reader in. Remember the line I used in Part 5?

"Bob set Jane onto the bed and lay down on top of her. Without a word he put his cock into her."

And we changed it to

"Bob threw Jane onto the bed and lunged on top of her. Without a word he thrust his aching cock into her."

So we added action words, right? (And "aching", which is description, which is what we're doing now.) But it's still not very good. So let's add more description— which is almost exactly the same as adding more emotion and sensation—to those two basic sentences. How's this:

Bob growled low in his throat and threw Jane onto the soft bed. The satin sheets cooled her fevered skin, but she barely had time to feel it before he lunged on top of her. Every inch of his hot, bare skin touched hers, made her sizzle with need.

He didn't speak. He didn't need to. Instead he shoved her thigh up, making room for his hips, and in one swift, smooth movement thrust his entire thick length into her slick heat.

Now again, this isn't great. (I feel bad giving you guys kind of generic crap examples, but there's a reason for it, which you'll find out this week or early next. Trust me). But it's much better, isn't it? Because it's more descriptive. Because it gives us some insight into what Jane is feeling, seeing, thinking. Because we're describing what's happening, the act of thrusting is given some weight; it becomes something we can experience along with Jane, not just something we're being told about.

Your sex scene should be descriptive. Describe everything for the reader. How hard is he? How wet is she? How desperate are they? What does everything feel like, look like, smell like, taste like? If you don't give the reader this information they won't be drawn into your scene the way they have to be.

So here is a list of descriptive words. None of these have to do with setting, because we're going to do setting separately along with POV.

swollen   oversensitive/sensitized   achingly sensitive (although again, being descriptive doesn't give you license to be lazy and fill your scene with telly adverbs)   slick needy   aching   desperate   hot   heated   hard   weeping velvety   waiting   shaky/shaking   trembling   glorious (there's a whole family of complimentary descriptions— gorgeous, beautiful, etc. etc.—use them!)   erect (nipples can be erect too, don't forget)   burning   greedy   smooth hard   turgid   tumescent   wide   thick   searing   rock-hard iron-hard   rampant   demanding   rigid   soaking delicate   tender   tender folds   delicate folds   glistening leaking   salty   musky   sweet   aggressive   raw   tight strong   heavy   tight   muscled

That's not a complete list, by any stretch. But it's a start, I hope; come up with your own as well!

The point is, nothing in a sex scene should just be *done*, unless it's for effect or fits the rhythm. In the little example above, Bob thrusts into Jane with one swift, smooth thrust, because the two sentences before the thrust were fragmentary so we needed something longer for the rhythm. If we'd had a longer sentence, perhaps a line of dialogue, or perhaps he was playing with her ladyparts or she was caught in swirling need or whatever, we could have just said "He thrust into her" and it would have been a great, strong declarative sentence—because it was surrounded by description elsewhere.

A sex scene should be fun to write, and it should be fun to read. Let yourself play with words, pile them on, build towers with them.

And it's not just about what their bodies feel like. It's not just about what they're doing. It's about how they're doing it. This goes back to the post about emotion and sensation; remember the two examples? One was pure action and rather dull. The other added

100

characters and all that good stuff and was (hopefully) much more effective.

Don't have your hero simply put your heroine on the bed. Give him a stronger, manlier action word ("manly" is an okay descriptive word too) and make her feel it. Don't just tell us he has a big cock; show the reader how the heroine feels about that by describing his big, gorgeous cock, and how thick it is or how threatening or how her mouth suddenly feels dry.

But you're not just describing body parts, you're describing actions. Every one of those actions has to have a purpose, and the way you show the reader that purpose is through description. He doesn't just touch her, he *glides his hand over her*. He doesn't just pick her up, he *gathers her in his big strong arms*. He doesn't get on top of her, he covers her with his body, he presses his wide, strong chest to hers, he crushes her under his delicious weight, he covers her with his warm living flesh. If he kneels before her, why does he do it? Is he looking at her ladyparts and licking his lips, erotic hunger glowing in his eyes? Is he kissing her thighs, nibbling the tender skin behind her knees (warning: some of us are very sensitive back there and get weirded out when it's touched. Just FYI.)

No movement should be basic. Basic is awkward. Basic is boring.

Action without description is bland, and it's dangerous in a sex scene. Just as in a real-life sex scene, you don't want to spoil the mood.

So. Go back to one of those published sex scenes you really like, and get out a sheet of paper or open a Word doc or whatever you like. Read the scene start to finish. Now read it again, this time writing down every descriptive word in the scene. Every adjective. Every adverb. Every strong verb (you can put them in separate columns or lists if you like). Do the same with a few other

101

scenes. Hey, if there's a scene you don't like, that didn't touch you in any way, do the same thing for it. Is there more or less description in that scene? What percentage of description seems to work for you—how much is too much (yes there is such a thing as too much! It's hard to reach but it is possible).

Now look at your own scenes. How much description do you use? Do you have as many words as the scene you liked? Are there any actions that have no description, and why? Is it for rhythm or is it simply because you didn't put any description in?

Now write a short new scene, but with a rule: You must use at least two descriptive words for every body part and every action. Don't worry about repeating them (but try not to if you can avoid it); don't worry if it sounds right or not. But you cannot put a cock on the page if it isn't iron-hard and slick with need. You cannot put a cunt on the page if it isn't weeping and oversensitive. Thrusts must be hard and desperate or gentle and tender, kisses feverish and frantic or slow and deep.

Let it sit for a while and re-read it. Compare it to your other scenes. Is it hotter? Does it work better for you?

You can go back and edit it, take out the words you don't like—obviously a sex scene where everything has exactly two descriptive words is going to read a bit metronomic. But it's a start, and hopefully it will make you more comfortable with using description.

Part 21, Sex: It's not just for bed

Just as we describe every movement in a sex scene—or almost every movement—and just as every movement has its purpose, so does setting. Your characters aren't just interacting with each other; they're interacting with what's around them, even if they're not actively doing so.

For example, in a bed, sheets may be soft or rough. They may float on top of the mattress or sink into the featherbed. They may fist the sheets, push them out of the way, burrow under them.

All those are pretty elementary, really, because let's face it. No matter how adventurous we may be, I think it's a safe bet that the majority of our sexual encounters take place in bed. We're all familiar with how pillows can be used to prop up bodyparts or bitten to muffle sounds. But what about other places? What do you grab when you're in a car, say, or up against a wall in an alley?

In *Day of the Dead*, Santos and Yelina have sex for the first time in a cemetery—on a bench beside his dead love's mausoleum, to be precise. And there were a few reasons why I chose this setting.

One, because the story is set on the eve of Dia de los Muertos, so I wanted to get as much graveyard imagery in as I could.

Two, because by having Santos break his seventy-two years of celibacy by his love's grave, I could add some guilt and thus emotional intensity and complication to the plot.

Three, because I could use it symbolically; death of the old love and birth of a new one (this worked especially well—not to toot my own horn—because I left some ambiguous little hints there that Yelina might be

103

the reincarnation of Esperanza. Just hints, and you can form your own opinion, but I liked that ambiguity and liked the extra depth it added to the story).

Four, because it gave me a chance to introduce grave-robbing, and who doesn't want grave-robbing in their erotic romance?

Five, because given the plot and general setting, it was a good place for the characters to run into each other—Santos would naturally go to Esperanza's grave on such an important holiday, and Yelina might reasonably choose to visit her father's grave on that night as well.

And six, because what writer doesn't want to write public sex in a cemetery at night? Seriously, that's hot.

But the point is, it wouldn't have been as hot if I'd just stuck Santos and Yelina in a graveyard for no reason. Just like you can't just stick your characters places for no reason.

We all know agents and editors dislike static settings. Why have endless pages of people sitting around in a living room or kitchen, drinking tea and chatting? (Yes, I know I'm guilty of overusing this in *Personal Demons*. Shut up.) Why not have that conversation on a rooftop (everything is better on a rooftop, trust me)? Or on a bridge? Or in a speeding car, on a beach, in an opium den, underground, in a dark alley, on a rusty fire escape?

You can't always do that, of course. In the middle of the night, when the characters are home, it makes no sense that after someone tries to break into their house and they defeat them, that they would then get dressed and put on coats to go find a rainy, rat-filled alley in which to discuss the break-in. But try to find more active settings, and that goes for sex as well.

Off the top of my head, here is a partial list of places where my characters, in all of my books, have had sex. I'm not putting bed in here, but pretty much all of them have had sex in bed at least once. Often more than once, but in different positions etc. So:

Hot tub
Hotel room floor
Bathroom counter
Graveyard
Up against a lightpost on the street
In a public park, hidden behind pine trees
Hot, dusty attic
On a desk in an office
On rocks by a waterfall
Up against a tree
On the beach
In a field
On a front lawn
Poolside chaise lounge
Shower
Forest clearing
Couch
Bedroom floor
Up against a wall in an alley
Up against a wall in a living room
In a museum
Workout room
Balcony
Nightclub
Cave
Bar bathroom

I might very well have missed some, but those are the ones I remember.

Now look at that list. Think about it. How do you imagine the sex up against the lightpost, on the public street, was different from a scene in bed? How might the hot, dusty attic be different from the forest clearing? The museum from the field? Picture those scenes as you imagine them. What are the difference?

See what I mean? Setting feeds action, and action feeds setting. When you're planning for your characters to fight and have angry sex, what setting would be best for that? You can have them fight anywhere, right? You don't have to start a fight in a bedroom just because there's a bed handy there. How much better to have them fight in a nightclub, which is already hot and too-close in atmosphere, and get so overwrought they end up in the hall, not caring who sees, Maybe they can even get busted for it, and add a huge complication.

Maybe you want them to be tender and romantic. Bed is a good setting for that, but how about the public park? How about putting the tender scene in the nightclub—how will you use the atmosphere differently then? Rather than being so angry they don't care who sees, they're so wrapped up in each other it's like no one else even exists. See?

You don't need to veer into cliché here. You don't want to do that. You don't want all your tender scenes to happen in the forest while the little bunnies watch and the little birdies chirp sweetly, or on a wrought-iron four-poster bed with flowy white sheets and sunshine pouring in. You don't want angry scenes to always take place during thunderstorms on fire escapes against rusty bars. But you can try those. Even better, mix them up, and let the reader feel the incongruity between action and setting. And don't just put them in a setting and forget about it. Just like you feel the bed beneath you or the wall cold against your back, so do they. You don't want to go overboard with it, of course—the focus needs to be on the sex—but interacting with the setting adds depth and reality to the scene.

For example, from *Day of the Dead*:

"Yelenita," he whispered, rolling her clit between his index finger and thumb until she wanted to sob out loud. "Yelenita, *mi amor*."

The stone of the bench scraped against her back, but she didn't care. Didn't care at all, because her thighs rested in his iron grip and his mouth descended on her pussy. A low, gasping groan escaped his lips, vibrating against her as he sucked her clit into his mouth. "Santos, oh God, Santos…"

The tree branches above her swayed dizzily in the breeze, the night air cooling her fevered skin as she trembled under his talented onslaught. He pulled back, teasing her with his tongue, then slipped one thick finger inside her, twisting it easily in her soaking channel.

So here we have the bench and the trees. I don't mention the setting again for a page or so, when we're back in Santos's POV and he's looking at Yelina:

And here she was, her smooth curves gleaming in the dappled moonlight coming through the trees above, her body warm and alive and full of promise in his arms, and he trembled as he took off his trousers and cool air swirled around his swollen cock.

But the setting is there; it adds a little flavor to the scene, it grounds the scene in its setting, so Santos and Yelina are people having sex in a place and not bodies floating somewhere. The setting becomes part of the scene, albeit a very small part, and that's what you want.

Your setting should be part of the scene; it should add to the emotion, heat, and intensity of the scene just like the words your characters say or the way they touch each other. It is a third, minor character in the scene. Don't neglect it.

I was going to do POV as well but this ended up being longer than I expected. So, here's the assignment. Take one of your sex scenes and move it to a different setting. It doesn't have to be sensible; this is just an exercise. But take the scene and remove all references to setting, adding a new one. This time, put the scene in any of the places I listed above.

How does the scene change? Does it at all? How does it feel working that new setting into the scene, does it gain or lose something? Is it more interesting or less?

Make your own list of places you'd like to write sex scenes, and keep it somewhere you'll be able to find it. Go through some of your unpublished work; how many scenes take place in a bed? How many of those can you change? Even changing the weather outside can make a difference; is it hot and sunny so the sun makes bright golden rectangles on the sheets and caresses their skin like a warm hand? Rainy, so they need to light up the room on their own? Snowy? Does the wind whistle around the corners of the building? Do they hear it over the roaring of blood in their ears or their own gasps and moans?

Think of a setting you've seen used particularly well, or not well. What was done right or wrong? What would you do differently?

Part 22: What are you doing to me?

The heat inside her roared like a beast, rising up into her throat and escaping as cry of pure, wanton delight. She'd thought last night she could never experience anything as wonderful as him on top of her, thrusting inside her. Now she knew she could. In this position, his balls thudded softly against her clit with every thrust.

She lifted her ass and spread her legs a little more, making it easier for his skin to touch hers. He was so hot, the thickness of him searing her insides, his pelvis warm against her behind. Slowly he danced out of her, rolling his hips so his cock touched every inch of her walls, then just as slowly crept back in. She rocked her hips against him, circling in the opposite direction, and the tightening of his fingers on her hips told her how much he liked it.

Royd slid one hand up her spine and looked down to watch himself sink into her body and reemerge, slick with her moisture. He would never, could never grow tired of that sight. He leaned back a little, bending his legs further to get a better view.

All the while, Prudence's sighs and gentle moans egged him on, told him what he wanted to hear. Her cunt was tight and hot around him, welcoming him with every thrust. He thought of the way those walls had felt around his tongue the night before and almost exploded. He wanted to taste her again, wanted to feel and explore every inch of her body.

What did you notice about that excerpt? Anything? Anything you want to comment on? Did you notice the POV switch?

I know conventional wisdom is to never, ever head-hop. And I agree, generally. It doesn't always bother me but I do notice it, and generally find it too "telly." It's not fun if you don't get to deduce things for yourself. (For example, in one of my books I have the heroine push the hair out of her face, close her eyes, and smile, feeling the breeze on her skin. When she opens her eyes the man she's with quickly looks away and busies himself with something. Hopefully it's obvious to the reader that he was watching her, probably open-mouthed with a stupid look of longing on his face [stupid to him, I mean] and that he's now embarrassed at almost being caught. I could easily have slipped into his POV for that and *told* the reader he was watching her and thinking she was the prettiest girl he'd ever seen up close, and that she was smart and brave and all that stuff too—or whatever sappy thoughts he was having at the moment—but I don't think that's anywhere near as much fun, do you? Or as interesting. [And yes, this paragraph is referring to Chess and Terrible on the cliff at the beach in UNHOLY GHOSTS, if you're curious. Remember, it hadn't been released yet when this was written.]

I like subtle clues, and I think readers like them too; it makes them feel smart, and I like to make readers feel smart, because it makes them feel engaged, and obviously that's the main goal, right? I digress.)

So generally, POV switches should have a scene break, or at least a line break (a blank space) between them.

Except for sex scenes. Or rather, except for some sex scenes. I know, you might not agree with me (ooh, I'm controversial!) but I think, if you're writing a book from multiple POVs or from both characters' POVs, you ought to have at least one sex scene where we get to see into both their heads. Generally that One Scene is the big "I love you" sex scene, because it's such an important moment that frankly I think the reader deserves to see into both people's heads. I also like to switch at some point during the First Sex scene, and one of the more emotionally charged ones in the middle—angry or frantic sex, say. Any sex scene that represents a huge leap or is emotionally fraught is a good place to let your reader see into both heads.

Like I said I know there are some who won't agree with me. It's also very possible your publisher will force you to put a line break in there to signify the switch. Personally I think if you do it right, the reader will hardly even notice; it will feel right and natural to them to see into both characters' heads, and it's for that reason I dislike the line break. I think it calls unnecessary attention to the switch and interrupts the flow of the scene. But it isn't that bad and like I said, I know it's a necessary evil at some houses, so there you go.

The point isn't *how* it should happen, not really. That's a matter of house style and what your editor wants. It's a matter of *whether* it should happen, and why.

Oh, and. Only one POV switch per scene, please. I used to switch back and forth more, but once should really be enough (unless you're writing a ménage, in which case you may want to dip into all of their POVs—they're generally longer scenes, so you have some room).

I like the switch, though. I like to show the reader that both characters are feeling the same thing, thinking the same thing. I like the reader to see how significant a moment this is for both characters. It gives the reader a more complete picture.

And it can really amp up the heat level, because, as in the example above, not only are we seeing/feeling what Prue feels, we feel it from Royd's POV as well. In a different scene we might experience her orgasm with her, then switch so we can experience it with him—and then we get his as well. It can extend a scene and give us more room to play.

There's another point to the quoted scene, as well, and that's detail. Detail is an important part of writing a good sex scene. We've touched on this quite a few times throughout the series; it's one of those topics that's too important to ignore but too big for its own topic, IMO.

Royd doesn't just pull out and thrust back in. He doesn't just look down. He *looks down to watch himself sink into her body and reemerge, slick with her moisture.* We're giving the reader that image; a feeling and thought to go with the action, especially in the next line when we learn *he would never, could never grow tired of that sight.* And to drive it home (no pun intended) he *lean[s] back a little, bending his legs further to get a better view.*

I could have simply said Royd looked down to watch himself fucking her, or whatever. And in a different type of scene that might work. But it's a little telly, and it's simply not very detailed.

Details *matter*. Don't just tell us or even show us what the characters are doing; show us *why*, and how they each feel about it. Every action has a reaction, yes, and you want to include that, but every action also has a *reason*.

Your hero doesn't just thrust into the heroine, he *thrusts into her, feeling her slick, hot walls grasp him.* Or *tighten around him.* Or *give under the pressure of his thrust.* Your heroine doesn't just feel him thrust into her, she *feels every inch of him sliding against her wet, sensitive skin, feels her body welcome him, feels her tight walls being invaded.* Just as Prudence, above feels *how hot Royd is, the thickness of him searing her insides, his pelvis warm against her behind.* He doesn't just pull out of her; *Slowly he danced out of her, rolling his hips so his cock touched every inch of her walls, then just as slowly crept back in.*

Later, as Prudence gives Royd a blow job, instead of simply touching herself, *her other hand slid[es] down into her panties, onto her incredibly sensitive clit. She moved farther down, slipping a finger into her cunt, drawing her silky moisture out to spread over her aching flesh.*

112

See? They don't stroke each other; *they stroke each other, their palms memorizing the planes and contours of the warm, living flesh beneath them.* They don't just kiss, *their mouths dance, their tongues tangle, devouring each other, breathless.*

The devil's in the details. Heh heh.

This weekend's assignment: First, check your own scenes. Have you used POV switches? How do you feel about them? Do you think they're in the right place? (I believe there are two places ideally suited for POV switches; one, immediately before or after he enters her, and two, immediately before or after somebody comes.)

Take one scene you're written solely from one POV, and add a switch (remember, when writing from the male POV, think about what this man would be thinking and what you want any man to be thinking during sex. It's okay if it's a little cheesy, this is just practice). Now rewrite it with the switch in the other direction—if the scene starts with her and ends with him, switch those around. And as always, the POV should be with whichever character has the most to lose emotionally, or will be changed the most. Obviously, if you're writing a historical and the heroine is losing her virginity, that moment should be hers. If your hero is breaking a vow of celibacy, that moment should be his.

Now, reread that scene, or any of your scenes. Have you described every action fully? Are we getting a complete picture? When he climbs on top of her, for example, is every his bare skin hot against hers, everywhere? Does she feel his erection against her thigh and shiver? Are either of them shocked, amazed, pleased, thrilled, to be so close to each other? How does she see him, when he does it? This sort of thing is especially important for movements that may otherwise be awkward; if you're not going to brush over it ("he stripped off his clothes") you need to go into detail ("His fingers

113

couldn't undo the buttons fast enough for her; she struggled to help him," that sort of thing.)

Part 23: When it's not supposed to be sexy

What I should have done here is asked Mark Henry to do a guest post on this. I didn't though, so you're stuck with me, flying by the seat of my pants. I'm warning you in advance; I'm not at all pleased with this one, so I'm sorry.

I've never really written a sex scene that wasn't supposed to be sexy. I have thought about it though. And I admit, there have been times where the evil little imp in me takes over and, in the middle of hot foreplay, I've been tempted to write some premature ejaculation in there, or a woman's frustration at not being able to reach orgasm, or a dog bite, or whatever. I've resisted the urges, but it is tempting.

The way I see it, there are two type of funny or unsexy sex scenes. There's the always-funny kind, meaning the whole thing is a joke from start to finish; and the gotcha kind, with a surprise humorous ending.

I believe there's a trick with Gotchas, and I believe the info in the rest of the series will help you. (Actually I believe the info in the rest of the series will help you write both.) The trick with a Gotcha is, the hotter the foreplay, the stronger the chemistry, the funnier the gotcha will be.

Here's a snippet from a sex scene in *As the Lady Wishes*. I've rewritten it a tad to include a Gotcha:

"I do. I am. I can barely keep from pushing you back on that bed and driving my cock between your legs, regardless of what you have to say about it," he said through gritted teeth, his eyes wandering to her slightly spread legs with a need that shook her to her core.

115

"Then don't keep yourself." Lila spread her legs just a little wider, a thrill of desire pounding through her bloodstream as she revealed her slick center to his hungry gaze. "That's what I have to say about it."

With a sound of surrender, Arthur was suddenly on top of her, his hot, powerful body pressing her into the bed. His mouth found her lips hungrily, this kiss different than any they'd shared so far. His movements were more demanding, forcing her to abandon herself to the strokes of his tongue, the bruising caress of his lips. Lila squirmed beneath him, her legs dangling off the edge of the bed, knowing she should be intimidated by the force of his need. His control was obviously slipping away, but the increasing rawness of his possession thrilled her. She found herself reveling in the sensation, intoxicated by the knowledge that she was driving him into this frenzy of desire.

"We have to slow down." He pulled back from her lips with obvious effort.

"I don't want to slow down, I want you inside me." Lila lifted her hips into his, snuggling his cock against her clit and moaning at how wild the feeling made her.

"No, we have to—aaaah!"

His body shuddered above hers, great violent jerks that shook the bed. Hot, sticky liquid spilled over her stomach, her thighs.

She looked up. His face was red, his eyes downcast. "Arthur?"

"Oh, damn…shit, Lila, I'm sorry, I—I was hoping that wouldn't happen again, I thought the medication would help, I—I'll get you a towel."

"It's—" she started to say, but he was gone, scampering out of the room before she had a chance to get the word out.

Lila fell back on the bed, waiting for her breath to return. Great. She hadn't been with a man in so long, and now she'd found a heart-pounding stud who couldn't keep it up long enough to finish the job.

She really was in hell.

Now, I know it's not uproariously funny—and you men are probably sniffing right about now that there's nothing funny about premature ejaculation, ever—but you see the point. The bigger the build-up, the harder the fall (that snippet is actually from about the third page of foreplay between these two.)

And it might not be premature ejaculation, either. Perhaps it could be something like this:

"Do you want me to take everything off, Cecelia?" His voice was still low, teasing her, enticing her with the promise of what he would do to her when he removed his pants.

She nodded, unable to look him in the eye. She knew that if he looked in her eyes he would see how desperately she wanted him, and how vulnerable that would make her.

"I didn't hear you, Cecelia," he said. "I asked if you want me to take off all of my clothing. Do you want me to do that?"

"Yes," she whispered.

"I'm afraid you'll have to speak a little louder," he said. His hands moved to his belt and removed it, then undid the top button of his pants.

"Yes," she said, a little louder. God, he was making her beg…and she loved it. It was turning her on in a way she'd never expected, never experienced before in her life.

He didn't reply, but tugged down his zipper and slipped out of his pants. He wore nothing underneath, she saw the top of a thick patch of dark hair, surrounding… She lifted her upper body from the bed, propped herself up on her elbows. His cock—was that even a cock?

This had to be a joke. She could barely see it. As big around as her pinky finger, not quite as long. She looked up to see him grinning wickedly at her.

"Here I come, Cecelia," he said. "Are you ready for me?"

Now, either of those would have still been amusing, made their points, without the big build-up. But I think the build-up adds to it, makes it more of a surprise.

Now the other type is harder, at least for me. But again, what you're aiming for is turning the tropes on their head. It may be funny or just unsexy; how far you want to go is up to you.

Think of those trigger words, all those evocative verbs and nouns. Now substitute things like "bony" for "broad" or "soft" for "hard". Think of silly things, unsexy things. So instead of this:

Her words were stopped by the warm pressure of his lips on hers.

There was nothing tentative about Daemon or his kiss. He obviously took for granted that she wanted this, despite what she'd said, and she realized he was right as she found herself returning the kiss with equal passion.

Her lips parted and his tongue found hers, teasing her with light strokes, diving in and out of her mouth. She followed it back into the warmth of his mouth, and gasped when he caught it with his teeth, biting just hard enough to send a shiver through her.

He freed her hair from the clasp that contained it at the back of her neck, running his fingers through it, tugging gently. The sensation made shivers down her spine.

She leaned into him, pressing herself against him. Her breasts crushed against his chest, her nipples so hard and tight she was certain he could feel them through the layers of clothing that separated their skin.

As if confirming this, he removed one hand from her hair and brought it down to cup her breast through her shirt, the thick pad of his thumb rubbing across the peak. She gasped against his mouth and shifted position a little to give him better access.

In response he pulled away completely. She started to protest, to reach for him, when he let go of her. His eyes gleamed.

"Tell me again," he said, his normally cool tones rough with need. "Tell me how you don't want me."

We have this:

Her words were stopped by the warm pressure of his lips on hers.

Too much pressure. Her head bent back; she tried to shift her mouth, get a better angle, but his hand in her hair held her fast. Her teeth cut into the delicate skin inside her lips. It hurt, but he wouldn't let her pull away, his unschooled mouth forcing itself onto hers, his fingers like iron bars digging into her neck.

His pelvis moved against hers, fast, like a dog humping her leg, while he pressed what he obviously thought was an impressive erection into her stomach. It felt more like a mini gherkin. She grabbed at his shirt to keep from falling over. That was a mistake. He seemed to take it as encouragement, and pressed even harder, faster, his head unmoving, little throaty growling sounds coming from deep in his throat.

She opened her mouth, desperate for air, but instead of the breath she needed his tongue invaded her, probing like a dentist's drill. Something wet ran down her chin and trickled down her neck. Was that...spit? Was he slobbering on her?

She tried to push back with her own tongue, only to have his teeth clamp down on it. Tears stung her eyes. That hurt, fuck, what was he doing? Was this some kind of joke?

"Elizabeth," he moaned. At least he had to release her tongue to do it, but before she could pull away he tugged at the clasp holding her hair. His watchband, heavy silver links, caught; pain shot through her skull as he pulled both the clasp and at least a dozen strands of her long blonde hair off her head. The clasp fell to the glass-topped table behind her with a clank. She cried out, raised her hand to the bald spot.

He dove in for another kiss, licking her chin like it was a fucking ice-cream cone, up over her mouth to her nostrils.

She put her hands on his shoulders, meaning to push him away, but he was too fast for her. His palm covered her right breast and squeezed like it was a bag of sand he needed to test for weight.

The final straw came when he reached around, grabbed her ass, and yanked her toward him. Her forehead smashed into his chin, so hard she saw stars. She heard what she thought was a strangled moan of pain, but when she looked up, his eyes were shining.

"If you think this is good, wait until I get you in bed," he said.

She sighed. This was going to be a long night.

I know these aren't the world's best examples. Like I said, this really isn't my forte; humor isn't something that can be taught the way basics can be. But hopefully this gives a basic idea, something else to think about when you're trying to write an unconventional sex scene.

So here's the exercises. Go back to one of the published sex scenes you picked for an earlier exercise. Now imagine what would happen if:

1. Premature ejaculation
2. Bed breaks.
3. Someone walks in on them
4. A priest walks in on them
5. One of their mothers walks in on them
6. Dog bite
7. Insect on someone's chest
8. Unfortunate bodily functions
9. Vaginal dryness
10. Can't get it up
11. Stuffed bra
12. Stuffed trousers
13. Sneezing fit
14. Small rodent in the bed
15. Pipe bursts in ceiling

Or whatever you like. Rewrite the scene yourself (it's not plagiarism or copyright infringement, it's an exercise you're doing for yourself and not showing it to anyone and all that stuff; use one of your own scenes if you prefer), using that list or anything else you can come up with.

Write your own scene, as silly as you can make it. Don't worry about realism. Just be funny. Make aliens land. Give the hero a rash. Whatever you want.

Part 24: Why isn't it working?

So you sit down to write your sex scene. You're confident. You've been reading my little lessons and thinking about what they mean to you, what you agree with or don't agree with, how they inspire or don't inspire you, whatever. (Remember, the point of the series wasn't to make you write a sex scene the way I do; it was to inspire you to dig into yourself and think about what *you* want your sex scenes to say, what *you* think is sexy, how *you* like to write them and what you like about them).

So you've got Bob and Jane kissing in the bedroom. They're getting pretty passionate. The time is right; you start taking their clothes off. Woo-hoo! Bob slide his hand over Jane's bottom; Jane moans; they fall to the bed, and...

The scene dies.

Huh?

Why isn't it working? You've got emotion in there, you've got some hot trigger words, you're all excited, but the words are flat. It's awkward. Rather than thrusting smoothly into Jane, you keep picturing Bob losing his erection. Or the doorbell ringing and it's Bob's long-lost wife with a shotgun. Or Jane suddenly really has to pee. The heat, the urgency, just isn't there, and Bob and Jane feel like cardboard cut-outs pressing their sexless forms against each other, rather than two fully-fleshed people being intimate with each other.

Calm down. This happens to all of us at one point or another. (Relax, it happens to other guys too.) And it's absolutely fixable.

First, are you sure you're in the right mood? I'm not generally an advocate of the "You have to be in the mood/have the right atmosphere to write" shit, not at all. In my mind, if you can't sit down and put decent words on paper no matter what when you have to, you still have work to do before you can call yourself a writer.

But sex scenes are a bit different, they are. Another erotic writer (unfortunately I can't recall who) once said that if your panties aren't wet when you're writing a sex scene, you're doing it wrong (substitute the appropriate corresponding metaphor for men). You should be at least somewhat aroused; you should be into the scene. *The scene should turn you on.* So if you're mad at everyone in the world and the kids are running around screaming (and kids are the one thing that will distract me while writing a sex scene; it's difficult to write enthusiastically about cocks when my little princesses are trying to get my attention to sing a Barbie song for me) maybe it's best to hold off on the sex scene. It's the one and only time I give myself permission to wait a few hours, or until the next day.

So that's a possibility, if the scene isn't working. Try getting yourself more in the mood. Have a glass of wine. Put some sexy music on the iPod. Watch a hot movie, maybe, or read a hot book, or, well, whatever gets you in the mood, up to and including actual physical action.

In my experience, I think a good 75% of the problem is lack of chemistry. Remember, *the time to write a sex scene is when your characters cannot wait any longer.* If you're feeling tepid, if they're feeling tepid, it's not going to work.

An example: My sex scene in *Personal Demons* just was not coming off right. Because I'd gotten horribly stuck for two weeks, I'd skipped the entire aftermath of what happened in the park and gone directly to the ball; the kitchen kiss wasn't in there. Perhaps I felt a little disconnected from Megan and Greyson, too, but to me they just didn't feel quite desperate enough yet.

So I went back, and wrote the kitchen kiss. In their first kiss, they stopped themselves; basically ignored that it had happened, and moved on. But the kitchen... I think (hope) it's fairly clear that had Tera not walked in, that would have gone a lot further. They were completely carried away. They didn't want to stop (and I didn't either; I had to make them and myself quit writing, and that's where you want to be. Again, the time to write a sex scene is when it's too hard not to write it; the action simply flows, and you have to force yourself to stop it). And it was from that moment that Greyson's behavior grew more possessive, or rather, that he started behaving as though sex was a foregone conclusion ("When I'm in your bed," etc.), and although Megan wasn't as bold as he was, she sure didn't argue.

The kitchen kiss did, for me (and again hopefully for the readers) what I needed it to do; it amped the chemistry, it put them in a position where they were actively seeking physical satisfaction from each other. Once that was in place, the sex scene flowed; it remains one of my absolute favorite sex scenes I've ever written.

It doesn't have to be a kissing or foreplay scene, though. I've gone back and added more dialogue, a touch, a look, a thought. Anything, to put sex a little more firmly in the characters' minds and make them spark. A little shared joke, an inadvertent compliment, anything.

So if the scene isn't working, that's the second thing to try. Go back and reread all the interaction between those characters. Is it everything it should be? Perhaps it is, but you've simply fallen out of the swing of it. Rereading may help you get back into it. Maybe you need to write another kissing scene; maybe it doesn't need to go into the book (I can't imagine why, but it's worth a try, if you really think you have all you can use.)

Okay, so it's neither of those things. Are you simply uncomfortable with writing sex? This is where some of the exercises we've done come in. Remember when you wrote a dialogue scene where the characters expressed their feelings, then translated that to action?

Dig that scene you wrote out, or write a new one. That's your roadmap for this scene; use it!

That "roadmap" will also be helpful if your problem is that the characters aren't behaving the way those characters would. A hard-boiled cop hero may get mushy, but he probably won't be entirely comfortable with it; are you giving him dialogue that doesn't fit him? A woman afraid of being vulnerable isn't going to react the same way as a woman who's never been hurt, are you making sure we see her fear?

Try changing the location, too. Nothing says they have to be in bed. Maybe they're so desperate they do it on the couch. Or in the car. Maybe they're in bed but instead of him on top, she gets on top. Or they fall on the floor. Don't be afraid to mix things up; it may unlock the problem and save the scene.

And if all else fails, remember you can always rewrite it. You can always fix it in edits, that's what they're for!

A sex scene is a microcosm of the entire relationship. It is the biggest and best opportunity you have to *SHOW, not tell* the readers what these people feel for each other, how they feel about themselves, and what makes their relationship works. Don't be afraid of it; embrace it, let yourself go crazy with it. You'll feel good about it and your readers will love it.

So here's some final assignments. Go back and reread everything you've done so far (if you've kept them). Can you tell which scene was written for which lesson?

Merge all those scenes together, taking a line from one, a line from another, a bit here and there. Reread your new scene. What do you think of it? How does it work for you?

Go to the bookstore and buy a book that interests you, one where you know there will be a sex scene (or grab a book from your TBR pile). Now read the sex scene, and only the sex scene. Make some notes. What does the sex scene show you about the characters, their relationship, the story itself? Who is the dominant one? Are they reckless go-getters, or are they more cautious? Are they in love or do they just really like/want each other? Record every impression you have.

Now read the book. Were you right?

This is our last installment, sort of. Next I'm just going to wrap things up.

And so...we come to the end

Technically this is part 25. Can you believe it? We've been discussing sex scenes for nine weeks. The series is over 40,000 words. And I still haven't covered everything, not in the sort of detail I'd like.

For instance, I forgot to warn you of the dangers of the word "felt" and how it removes the reader from the action instead of placing them in the thick of it (as it were). When you say "She felt his hands move up her back" or "He felt how smooth her skin was" you're telling, not showing; you're pushing the reader away from those feelings. How much better it is to say simply "His hands slid up her back" or "Her skin awed him, so smooth and soft beneath his fingers." The only time you'd use felt is when you have no choice, or when you say being in his arms made her feel safe, or something along those lines.

I ran out of time before I could get heavily into the mechanics of ménage scenes. I could probably do another several thousand words on inserting emotion into your scenes, on using them to build character. I haven't shown you all of my examples. I didn't get into BDSM at all, and I had plans for that one—I still may do it, because I have a friend who is a lifestyle submissive and she'd agreed to do an interview for me. So look for that one, because I feel I've cheated her and you by not getting to it.

But for the moment, anyway, we're done. There are bits and pieces I've left out, sure. But I'm also conscious of the dangers of overexplaining things, of becoming redundant and boring. And to be honest, that worries me the most. I started the series because I thought it would be fun for me to do—which it absolutely was—but also because I thought I had something new to say on the subject, or at least, I have a different way to say it.

To that end I've tried to keep the series fun; I've tried to work at least one good joke into every installment, to make it so even if you're not a writer, or you don't write sex in your books (which, shame on you! Ha ha) you might have still enjoyed reading these. I wanted to encourage people who are nervous about or uncomfortable with writing sex scenes that it's fun, it's something you really can do.

It's just sex, guys. It's 100% risk-free sex, too; no actual bodily fluids are involved, at least not on the page (for me anyway; if you get actual bodily fluids on your pages, that is of course entirely your business. Freak).

And most of all, that there is nothing dirty about writing sex. That *a writer's job is to tell the truth*, and that the fact is, the deepest truths of our characters can be found when they are naked, when they are at their most vulnerable both physically and emotionally, when they let their guards down and just interact. Not every book requires a sex scene, of course, but there's no reason to shy away from them if yours does.

Let's put it this way. Perhaps I'm the only woman in the world who felt like this, but when I told my father that the hubs and I were expecting our first child, as much as I was excited and proud and all of that, I have to admit to one brief, fleeting moment of nervousness: He knows I've had sex! He's my *Dad*, and he knows *I'm not a virgin anymore*! (The fact that at the time of my marriage I was twenty-six years old and had lived with a previous boyfriend for two years meant nothing; I think he and I both pretended the ex and I slept in separate beds.)(Ooh, that reminds me of a funny story, which further illustrates the point. Annette Funicello, Disney's first squeaky-clean teen, said once in an interview that she often had people come up to her in public and say things like, "Annette, I can't believe you're smoking! I can't believe you're drinking!" Her response? "Well, I have three kids, so guess what else I do." Which, awesome. Anyway.)

So I was nervous about this, and actually had occasion one night, when we'd both had a few drinks, to mention it. And he just kind of shrugged and smiled and made some comment about how he'd thought I was artificially inseminated and where was that husband of mine so he could kill him for soiling his precious little girl. And that was what happened to my first husband. No, of course I'm joking! *Nobody* threw any bodies into the Everglades, *of course not!* Actually, he did think it was funny that I would even think that, and basically said, "Well, you're married; it's different when you're married."

And it's the same with books. It's different when you're writing books (whether you're married or not doesn't matter, it's just an analogy). It's not you. It's nothing to be embarrassed about. If people are reading your books, and wondering if it's a true-to-life encounter you're describing, that's their dirty-minded, inappropriately nosy little problem, just like people who wonder whether or not a bride "had the right to wear white." Only the nastiest sort of person would think this way; polite people don't speculate on such matters, which are none of their business (no, I will never stop working etiquette lessons into my blog posts. It makes me happy. Give me a break).

Anyway, we're done here. And I'd love it if you guys could do me a favor. Tell me what you liked best. Tell me if it helped you. Tell me if there was something I didn't cover enough, something you wished I'd cover but didn't. What was your favorite part, what helped you the most? What did you learn about your scenes and the way you write them, if anything? How? Do any of you look at writing sex scenes differently now? Do you feel more confident? Did you do any of the exercises, and if so did you find them helpful?

I'd really love the feedback. Either way, I can't thank you enough for reading this, and I sincerely hope you found it helpful and fun. Big hugs to all of you.

Made in the USA
Lexington, KY
12 September 2012